WARHAWK

AN EVANS NOVEL OF THE WEST

R.C. HOUSE

M. EVANS AND COMPANY, INC.
New York

M. Evans & Company, Inc.
216 East 49th Street
New York, New York 10017

Library of Congress Cataloging-in-Publication Data

House, R. C.
　　Warhawk / R. C. House.
　　　　p.　cm. — (An Evans novel of the West)
　　ISBN 0-87131-727-3 : $16.95
　　I. Title. II. Series.
　PS3558.0864W37　1993
　813'.54—dc20　　　　　　　　　　　　　　　　　92-21237
　　　　　　　　　　　　　　　　　　　　　　　　　　　　CIP

Typeset by AeroType, Inc.
Manufactured in the United States of America

9　8　7　6　5　4　3　2　1

For Doris

Who put up with a lot
for the sake of my "creativity."
I love you!

Chapter One

Jacob Lyman's sleep had been light; it was more than the cold.

Someone was out there camping on his trail. The intruder had been out there for days, bewildering Lyman with his behavior, keeping the trapper always on guard. Skinned beaver carcasses had been stolen when he was out checking his traps. The faint smells of distant cook fires and roasting meat told a confusing story.

There seemed little to do, he thought, but wait for the next move; and be prepared for it. The attack could come at any time.

Lyman reluctantly inched his head out of the snug coil of buffalo robe that had encased his body during the frigid night. The land sloping to the distant mountains and the trees near him were cloaked in silence, a closed-in kind of stillness that could only come when the chilling ground fog clung to the land, as it did this morning.

Dead or slow-moving water would be capped with a glaze of ice, sketched with fern-line wrinkles. But over it all, the land eternally held a crystalline beauty, winter or summer. In its vastness was more than a man could absorb maybe in a lifetime, full of awesome and strange distances that would be just as beautiful as those left behind when he came to the end of them. Lyman's days in the mountains had been stamped with that kind of incredible glory.

The cold snap had quickly turned the beaver pelts prime, giving him good cause to be out in this inhospitable weather. By comparison, summer fur was scraggly and thin. Now the pelts were heavy with long, sleek guard hair, the downy underfur thick and rich as cream.

Lyman's years in the mountains had taught him that the day probably would not warm up much more than it was at dawn. "Get out of the robe now or never, Lyman," he grumbled aloud, his sleep-slitted eyes hunting the area around him for any sign of his unwelcome companion or companions.

No point, he thought, in running from them. They probably lurked out there huddled like him against the cold. For most of a week, Lyman knew he was being watched. Probably a lone Indian, the sign seemed to say; maybe two. Possibly they were outcasts from a nearby village who may have violated some code or other.

*Some*one coyotin' around out there, for sure, he thought. Probably not so much waiting to give me an Indian haircut as to make free with my possibles. That was what made it all so infernally bewildering and irritating.

Jake Lyman had Indian friends far to the west, over the range. Other white trappers would winter in that village as well. It did not fit Lyman's scheme to go there this year. He proposed that when the weather forced him to take cover, he'd build a small, snug shanty, fill it with meat while he could still move through the country, and ride out the long and bitter-cold months alone until coming-grass time.

Heading for his string of beaver sets, Lyman eyed the neatly stacked pile of five grinning, naked, and red beaver carcasses trapped the day before. He was certain that when he returned about midday, one or two of the stiffening hulks would be pilfered. That seemed to be all his stalkers wanted— for now. Perhaps later they'd become bold and make their move to relieve him of his rifle and fixings, and his horses. And maybe his life.

The sun was little more than a small circle of brilliance at its meridian in a cold, clear sky when Lyman trudged back toward his camp. His heavy, big-bore rifle tugged at his right arm. A fat beaver strained at his left arm and hand, gripped by the convenient hold where the thick tail met the body. Over his shoulder, on thongs that bit into his flesh, dangled three animals. He judged his load at more than a hundred pounds.

Nearing his camp, Lyman was abruptly alert. He was not certain if it was smell or sound; there was an imperceptible bit of both in his sense of sudden alarm. Lyman stuck out his nose, feeling for scent like a dog.

He easily dropped the beaver from his left hand and shrugged out of the thongs holding the others. Leaving them, he faded into the woods beside the cleared stretch that passed for a trail. He would approach his open camp area from the trees, keeping well hidden.

Quietly, taking his breath in short, choked sobs, Lyman moved in a crouch from tree to covering tree, his big rifle at the ready. Ahead he could see the sky through the web of limbs above him, sign that he was nearing his camp clearing.

He paused at the edge of it and surveyed the scene. An Indian crouched at the pile of dead animals, back to Lyman, butchering a beaver carcass and piling chunks of meat on what looked like a canvas or cloth square for easy carrying. The Indian was slight of build, and short. Possibly a youth or older boy.

He wore a deer hide like a cape, the hair in some places falling out from poor treatment; hardly proper protection for this weather. A grey scrap of shawl was tied around his head for warmth.

Somebody down on his luck, Lyman thought. A poordevil at that, an Indian nobody wants. Huh! Wellsir, I'll just sit tight and let him take what he needs of the meat. Let him have the damned festering beaver if that's all he wants.

Movement at the other side of the clearing caught Lyman's attention. The bushes shook as though someone or something was moving. Well, Lyman thought, what have we here? There's that one's pard, or I'm poor bull. Lyman stayed in his tense crouch, every muscle tight with alertness.

A snout the size of a log of grey stove wood charred at one end poked through the brush. That was followed by a great, gray head, the breadth of a man's hips between the tiny, inquisitive eyes.

"Damn!" Lyman grunted. "Grizzly!"

His jaw dropped in surprise as the bear lumbered into the clearing tracing the scent of the stack of dead beaver. The monster, its great, gray humped back towering behind its head, stopped, also in surprise, at the smell of the human squatting at the pile of meat.

Instantly Lyman cursed himself for not being more careful. The bear, in its marathon feeding ritual before hibernation, was drawn to the smell of aging meat. Anyone near such meat, especially someone unaware, was in danger. The bear moved toward the Indian in a pigeon-toed lope, moving fast.

Whipping up the rifle, Lyman shouted a warning at the Indian. He held his fire. If he shot and only wounded the bear, the animal's rage would be doubled. At Lyman's shout, the bear bellowed an ear-splitting howl of animal anger. The Indian bounced to a surprised, upright crouch, turning to see the massive animal nearly upon him.

It was chancey, but it had to be done. Lyman brought up the rifle and took aim. As he did, the bear rose, towering on hind legs twice as tall as the pitiful Indian who shrank back in a paralysis of terror, unable to move.

Lyman lifted his sights, aiming for the area just behind the tiny puff of hair that was the grizzly's ear. The gun was a .60 caliber, its bullet rammed down on a load of powder that would pack a killing wallop into even such a diehard target as this massive silvertip.

The bear pounced on its victim, cuffing the man aside. The long, flexed claws sent the deer hide sailing, their razor-sharpness raking the man's chest. The Indian was lifted off his feet and flung aside; the bear dropped again to all fours, its cavernous jaws gnashing, reaching out for a death grip on the tiny head. The massive jaws could crunch it like an egg.

Coolly, Lyman followed the bear's moving head over the rifle sights. He laid the front blade low in the buckhorn rear behind the tiny cup of hair-covered ear and fired. The air filled with the belch of explosion and the cloud of rifle-smoke.

The bear's flews, curled back from giant fangs, relaxed and sagged. The animal stood bewildered, without moving, as though wondering what had made the sudden sound and incredible hurt. The bear swayed a moment on its stubby legs, its entire body rocking. It leaned away from the fallen Indian and dropped with a resounding thud like the crash of a big tree.

Lyman rose slowly, watching the scene before him. The Indian lay unconscious a few feet from the quivering pile of muscle and fur that was the dead or dying bear. Wary through seasoned eyes, Lyman deliberately lifted his powder horn, measured a charge and stoked the rifle from the fixings in his beaded hunting pouch.

His tingling body quieting now, Lyman looked again at the scene in the clearing. The ground fog was completely gone; his view of the two bodies was clear. The Indian and the bear lay silent. Slowly, the trapper stalked out of the encircling trees, rifle at the ready. He took no chances. He was also pleased with his shot. The grizzly was obviously dead, the spinal cord severed at the base of the brain. A quick, clean kill was a soul-satisfying kind of kill.

As the trembling tension of the confrontation flowed out of Lyman, it was replaced quickly by a soaring, visceral kind of pride in the accomplishment. Grizzlies were the toughest animals in the mountains to kill. They died hard. More than a few men had gone down in encounters with them. Lyman's killing of this giant had been almost easy. He knew he would savor these moments of victory for the rest of his life.

Lyman laid the animal's resistance to its great reserves of vitality and power. Still he covered the ground slowly. The bear could be up in an instant and tear out Lyman's throat, or crunch his skull to pudding as it had tried to do to the Indian. Lyman studied his quarry. The huge hide, taken at its prime, he would tan with the bear's brains mixed with water. Later he'd smoke it, Indian-style, over a smudgy fire for a rich softness. The hide would become a thick, warm carpet for his winter quarters.

But, oh my God, Lyman thought, what a skinning job! He would have to forget the trapline for a day with the skinning and butchering of the great beast.

There was the problem, too, of the Indian. Was he still alive? Lyman would have to attend to him right away. He approached the two forms cautiously. They still lay silently in the clearing. He checked the grizzly first. The eyes were open, glazed in death. The black, inquisitive nose, cross-hatched with tiny wrinkles, was turning dry. Lyman knew that his bullet hole would be deep in the fur behind the ears.

The Indian lay on his stomach, his faced buried in the ground-mat of twigs and grass. Lyman had nothing to fear now. He squatted beside the body and gently lifted it, turning the man on his back. Feeling the arm and back muscles, Lyman knew the man – or boy – still lived. At least for now.

The face, framed in the shred of shawl, was petite with no whiskers or hair-fuzz. Had it been a woman, she would have been termed attractive. The black hair he could see under the shawl was parted in the middle, Indian-style. The skin and gentle features, however, did not seem to be that of an

Indian. It was more that of a swarthy white, tanned by exposure; it did not have the typical red Indian cast.

The man's blood-soaked shirt was faded and threadbare. Once a red-and-white check designed to be warm, it had been worn too long and washed a few too many times by beating on a rock beside a stream. He wore faded gray linsey-woolsey trousers and moccasins. The shirt was no longer worth wearing. The bear's claws had shredded it from one shoulder, across the chest, tearing the buttons free, and along the breast into the side.

Lyman carefully raised part of the shirt, heavy with blood, and gasped. Three lacerations ran deep as knife cuts from the man's shoulder and down across the chest, still oozing blood. They would need treatment if the man was to live. Long and lumpy purple scars would be evident for a lifetime. Lyman peeled back the side of the shirt to expose the slashed flesh and gently lifted it off the wound.

"Judas Priest!" he said aloud. The bear's great claws had raked across an ample breast. It was a woman! Lyman quickly studied her face again. She was white.

He leaped up and headed for his buffalo robe and camp gear in the rocks. The woman would need immediate attention.

An hour later, Lyman had cleansed the wounds, laboriously stitching them with a fine needle and thin sinew. His clean, blousy calico shirt, saved for special occasions, had to be sacrificed for bandages. The woman remained unconscious. Her face had flushed and turned feverish. He bathed her cheeks and forehead with cloths dampened at the river and tried to make her comfortable. Treating an injured person, particularly a woman, was a new experience.

Her fever abated by late afternoon. Lyman wrapped her in the buffalo robe. There would be no choice when darkness fell. He must roll up and sleep with the woman in his only article of bedding.

Dusk was again limiting his vision when he rekindled his fire not far from the great hulk of dead grizzly lying on its side, reflecting the firelight. He decided against cutting into the carcass for meat until he could properly skin the bear. Lyman had taken the time to gut and bleed the great animal to protect the meat, which would make many a fine meal.

He had disposed of the offal, as well as the rigid corpses from old beaver catches. No point in risking another grizzly confrontation. He warmed more of his supply of venison and gnawed on it for his dinner.

He heaped his fire higher, taking as much of its warmth as possible into his body, hoping the fire would warm the woman, an unmoving bulk under the heavy robe. The night, as expected, turned cold.

Knowing he would have a devil of a day's work ahead of him, Lyman gritted his teeth and worked his way into the robe with the woman. He had known women before, St. Louis riverfront women, and any number of squaws at rendezvous and when wintering over in friendly villages during his years in the high country. This was different.

"Forget it, Lyman," he thought. "This is ridiculous."

But instinct, he also told himself, was a powerful force. Aside from his year trapping with Rene Lamartine, Lyman had been a loner—always sufficient unto himself. In recent years, though, as he sensed he was approaching that maturity of manhood that comes with three decades, more or less, there had often been thoughts of a woman.

A woman to call his own; one to understand his life's tasks, to talk with, to share his dreams.

But who was she? Who was this one he held tenderly in his arms like a sleeping wife? A relaxing warmth spread over him, turning him drowsy. It had been a hell of a day. Still, racing thoughts tormented him, keeping him from sleep. In spite of the strangeness, the feel of the woman in his arms was good.

Was she an escaped captive of the Indians? The signs pointed that way. Maybe she had been wed to a brave killed in battle and with his death had become an outcast. Someday he'd know.

He would have to keep her with him during the long and bitter-cold months ahead. Circumstances obligated him. That resolved, Lyman's mind calmed and his brain drifted off toward dreamless sleep.

Chapter Two

Not so the woman he held in a clumsy, self-conscious embrace. She was barely conscious of her injuries. Mercifully the trauma of the grizzly attack had slammed her into a subconsciousness that left her senses dangling between hallucination and total oblivion. She was aware of a burning on her skin, not from fever, but from the memory of the intense sun that bore down on the military escort that afternoon of the fatal attack on the army wagon train.

Recollection was a blistering bright orange haze, diffused and fuzzy at the very edges of her senses. It phased gradually to startling clarity at the center, bright and graphic like looking down a golden, dazzling tunnel. These were the odd moments of memory before the Indian attack when time hung suspended, the moments before the screaming and the panic blasted out of the stark concussion of battle; before the great paralyzing blows of terror resounded like thunder deep inside her. Those moments before the attack were engraved on her memory-eye like the etched words of poignant grief on a granite tombstone.

Her husband, Second Lieutenant Edwin England, riding back to her and their young son, Daniel, in the military ambulance. Little Daniel, only twelve, resting his still-warm forehead against her breast with her arm around him; little

Daniel recovering from a week-long bout with the trail fever that nearly claimed him.

Edwin, once so handsome and resplendent in his dress uniform at West Point in fatigue blues, his bearing militarily proper on his blooded mare, a graduation gift from his parents; Edwin swinging back to the ambulance, his face flushed with heat and stress, the folds of his uniform liberally dusted with the grime of the trail.

Rachel's heart felt a pang for the drawn expression of Edwin's features; for each line, each taut point of his face tracing the strain of responsibility for safely taking the small contingent of dragoons, and his family, across the endless expanse of monotonous land to his first post of military authority.

Momentarily the vision vanished. Rachel abruptly knew cold. It was hard to remember being warm. Still her body was afire, feeling the frailty of fever stretching to every part of her. Then the chills returned, but quickly she became aware of the comforting warmth of fur enclosing her, replacing for a moment the fire of fever. A robe enveloped her with its snugness, that very feeling working a miracle in her torn body. A warm, masculine form wormed its way in with her in this cocoon of comfort, and she sensed the reassurance of strong, protective arms circling her body, now weak and limp with fever. Somehow she felt it was Edwin; her hallucinating mind allowed the illusion.

"Edwin," her lips formed the words, but no sound came. "Edwin! It's really you, after all! Oh, my dearest, I'm so relieved."

But Edwin was dead, she knew. She'd seen him after the massacre and her capture. The shock of reality drove her again into the terrifying web of hallucination. Out of the haze of glaring and suffocating sun the savage horde had come, thundering in assault from the west, taking form out of the blinding blaze of afternoon sun ahead of the troop. Bare-

11

chested, unclothed, bronzed barbarians charging in on giant horses to surround Edwin's troop with thuds of shock and terror and screams ramming into Rachel's senses.

Edwin's dragoons, hopelessly outnumbered, were strung out and totally disorganized in the rout to escape. Edwin's screamed commands to regroup, straight out of his training at the Point, knifed into her brain. He had been near the ambulance when the attack hit. Over the frenzy of thunderous hoofbeats and dust, panicked screams and belches of gunblast, Rachel heard Edwin's shouted command stopped in mid-word.

She could not see the front of the wildly careering, bouncing ambulance and its driver; he could have been dead, the horses stampeding unguided. The large war party rode alongside the troopers and the train of wagons, picking off easy targets among the bunched-up fleeing dragoons.

The ambulance skidded to a halt. Out of the swirling dust of its wake, a savage face, contorted in fury and bloodlust, materialized at the open back of the ambulance wagon. Rachel shrieked in raw terror, clutching Daniel to her. Other twisted faces appeared, leering at their unexpected find. The young mother and her son were rudely plucked from the ambulance by coarse, brutal hands.

The moments fused into bursts of bone-jarring panic. Around her, troopers battled valiantly in futile resistance; hoarse shouts and screams filled Rachel's ears. Arrows whistled in the air, some socking with dull thuds against the ambulance near her.

Within the perimeters of her distorted vision, a wounded dragoon rose groggily on hands and knees in the rutted dirt. An Indian rushed up, bringing down his war-hawk as he came. The soldier's head opened with a melon-slushy whack and he fell forward amid the circling of roaring chaos.

As she was rudely propelled away from the wagon against her will, Rachel's hearing became a fading series of echoes.

12

Daniel's shrill, pleading voice crying "Mama! Mama! Mama!" and her own voice crying out in anguish to him, at first peaked sharply and then slid away as though she were falling slowly down a long, dark hole.

Screaming mindless screams, Rachel was roughly dragged away from young Daniel. Urged along by the vise-like grip on her arm, she staggered past the body of a young dragoon with second lieutenant shoulder scales lying faced down in the battered and bloody ground. His red, naked skull, scalped even to the ears, glared like a great, globular sore under the unrelenting blaze of sun.

Despite her terror and inability to focus her thoughts, Rachel was aware of blue-green clots of flies shiny with bloat already swarming over the ruby-mottled skull.

The nightmare faded into the dark oblivion of grateful sleep. The warm, comforting softness was all around her again. Her nose was tickled by the smooth, strong, but good smell of fur. The little girl within her wanted to giggle. Here and there, small stabs of cold crept into her body; they were of little consequence. Over it all she was snug in Edwin's strong arms again. When she awoke, Edwin was gone, taking love and warmth and security with him.

"Edwin," she called. "Edwin, where are you!"

"It's all right," a voice said, consoling her. It was a strange voice — not Edwin's — but soothing, and she was inclined to trust it. "You've had a bad wound, a bad time of it, ma'am. You'll be all right now."

Remembering the terrifying nightmare, Rachel abruptly cringed away from the sound of the voice, trying to make herself small in the robe. "Edwin? Is Lieutenant England all right, trooper?"

"Ma'am, I'm sorry. There's no Edwin here. Just you and me. I'm sorry."

Rachel's eyes flicked open through a curtain of tears. The blazing heat of the sun was gone, replaced by the enveloping

13

gauze of cold morning ground fog. The face looking down at her was chiseled, virile and concerned. The bearded man wore a fur cap and a bulky, hooded blanket coat, looming over her like a shadow against the sky.

"Not that it'll make much difference so soon, ma'am, but the name's Lyman. Jacob Lyman. I saved you from the grizzly yesterday, ma'am."

The nightmare of the savage massacre of Edwin's soldiers was still too vivid for Rachel to remember yesterday, yesteryears, or any grizzly attack. Somehow she knew the nightmare hadn't ended. There was a time of nightmare, a long period of terror that somehow she'd deal with in a minute. It was a nightmare she'd lived with for five long years.

"I'll fix some proper food for you directly, ma'am," the man said. "When you're up to it. And not spoilt beaver either. Some good deer meat."

Rachel didn't answer but allowed her eyelids to droop shut and she easily drifted back into the soft web of sleep.

True to Lyman's predictions, skinning out the grizzly was a hell of a job for one man. He brought his horses down to help roll the great hulk as he carefully pared the heavy hide away with his skinning knife. The pack horse, at first skittish from the smell of the dead killer bear, pulled with Lyman's calming words. Slowly the massive folds of hide yielded under his knife bearing lightly against the connecting membrane. He was careful not to cut into flesh nor score the precious hide.

He paused briefly in his morning-long chore to check on the injured woman. She was sleeping peacefully, though he remembered that her sleep in the night had been feverish and troubled. Her small face was beautiful in repose. Lyman's palm, pressed tenderly to her forehead, found it warm but not hot, sign that sleep was greatly aiding her recovery.

Lyman spread the giant grizzly hide on a flat, remote part of his clearing. It was nearly as large as a buffalo. He pegged

14

down the edges before getting busy cooking some meat for the sleeping woman.

From his packs, Lyman dug out his coffee and boiling pot and made some for the two of them. He tried to broil her venison chunk carefully, thinking she'd prefer it tender throughout. When it was ready, he wakened her.

"Ma'am," he called, touching her shoulder lightly so as not to alarm her. "Ma'am. Sure wish I knew your name."

She woke with a start. "Daniel? Daniel, where are you, dear?" Her wide, waking eyes were full of questioning and terror.

"Just me, ma'am. Jake Lyman. I've got some meat done for you . . . and some coffee. It's all I've got, but it'll do you good. Here, you take my capote." He covered her with the great hooded blanket coat, radiating warmth from his body.

Gradually, reality dawned on Rachel England. There was that great pain in her chest and shoulder. For some time she had been aware of it, but now came to grips with how it had happened.

"I remember . . ." she said. "I remember." Her voice now trembled with the pain.

"Good," Lyman said. "Get up. Here, I'll help." With the coat's warm bulk over her chilled shoulders, Lyman helped her closer to the fire. A cup of coffee already poured a thin steamy vapor to join the rising pillar of smoke. Lyman pared off a good-sized chunk of meat, impaled it on his knife-point and offered it to her.

"May I ask, ma'am, your name?"

She studied him as she chewed. Jacob Lyman was handsome in a rugged, substantial sort of way, every bit as reliable looking as Edwin England. When she had swallowed, she said, "Rachel . . . Rachel England."

"Would I appear bold if I spoke to you as Rachel?"

Without responding, she paused, but nodded. "I remember the bear now. You killed it?"

15

"It attacked you. Gave you a bad wound." Rachel sensed through Jacob Lyman's clipped awkwardness that when he warmed to knowing a person, the warmth in his manner of speaking would also emerge.

She tried to smile, remembering an upbringing that she had all but forgotten in five years of Indian captivity. "No one needs to tell me that, Mr. Lyman." She said it pleasantly, enjoying her first civilized conversation in what seemed ages. "The pain is making itself abundantly evident. I must have a look at it later."

"As you will. I'm sorry Miss Rachel. I had to care for it . . . stitched the worst places . . . did what I could. I did nothing improper. You'll probably need my help to dress it as it heals."

Such gentility seemed almost alien to Rachel after the years of Indian captivity. The smile she gave Lyman was another rare experience; she couldn't ever remember smiling. After the shock of the disaster wore off, there was no emotion; only the dull ache of desperation and depression. Secretly there had been tears, hidden from her captors. Her last smile, she recalled, had been over young Daniel's recovery from the trail fever.

"It's my turn to be sorry, Mr. Lyman, for not responding properly to your kindnesses. Your concern, really, is foreign to me. But welcome nevertheless. I haven't had anyone worry about propriety where I've been concerned for nearly five years."

"You've been an Indian captive." His question was more a statement.

"All that time. I managed to escape during a storm more than a week ago. I've been wandering ever since, trying to find someone I could trust. God, in his infinite mercy, seems to have finally delivered me."

"Forgive me if I seem to pry, Miss Rachel. You mentioned two names when you were waking up. . . ."

"Five years is a long time, Mr. Lyman. Edwin, my husband, was second lieutenant of dragoons. He was bringing me, with his command, to his new western assignment, a frontier post. He was killed, with all his men, in an attack by the Indians."

Lyman seemed unwilling to pry further.

"Daniel—the other name—is my son."

"Is? Where is he?"

"I don't know. He was twelve. He was taken from me during the battle. I'm confident he's alive, otherwise I wouldn't have been able to live out the years. I don't know where he is. Probably taken to another Indian village. I've not seen or heard from him since."

Lyman was thoughtful a long moment. "I'm afraid we'll have to winter here—or near here. Come spring, I'll get you to an army fort or one of the fur posts."

"Where are we?"

"Deep in the Shinin' Mountains, ma'am. A bit west of Green River."

Chapter Three

In the days that followed, with winter settling in with a penetrating chill, Lyman built the woman a snug cabin only a few miles from the camp of the grizzly attack.

Across the river and against the base of the mountains that would block the fury of the winter storms, Lyman discovered a natural cave extending into the mountain ten or so feet. It led off a grassy, tree-studded bench of about an acre, easily defended if need be. He couldn't be approached from behind, and couldn't be blind-sided except with difficulty on the part of attackers. Any kind of assault would have to come head-on, and his vantage point in that regard was near perfect.

A mountaineer had to take these things into account. Still, Lyman thought, with a cabin here, his front yard would take in considerable territory.

The cave's ceiling was irregular, but he could stand in most of it. More than a water or wind cave, this was a great fissure in the mountain—a roughly triangular adit with a floor that, with the removal of rocky debris, would provide a sufficiently flat, packed-gravel floor.

It had the look of having been a hibernation den for wintering bears, possibly even the grizzly whose hide would soon grace this same floor. Lyman was confident after that victory that he could stand off any critter, two- or four-legged, wanting to contest his squatter's rights.

At the rear of the darkened opening into the mountain, roughly off to one side, a vent ran skyward. He couldn't see out when he craned his neck to look up this shaft, and this suggested easy passage of smoke without allowing in the elements.

In his first exploration of the cave, Lyman built a fire, seeing the smoke curl freely out the natural chimney. Where the smoke issued out of the mountain he didn't know. He also knew it would probably disperse and not be a beacon for unfriendly eyes that might be surveying the neighborhood.

He came out of the giant cleft in the mountainside feeling pleased and proud. Lyman looked about him, stretching himself with the joy of having found the place. Trees grew up to the entrance. He would only have to remove a few to extend his cabin out past the opening. Some sort of log extension of the cave was surely called for. He could even curtain off part of it for the woman's privacy and her own sleeping quarters. He had spied one nook of the cave that would be perfect for that. He dreamed it with that in mind.

There was enough fallen wood under the trees roundabout to keep them in fuel during the lost days of winter. His mind's eye visualized it. One giant pine blocking the cave's entrance would make a fine ridgepole for the cabin extension of his dugout. Others would suit for roof purlins and wall logs for the sides. He'd give the roof sufficient pitch to hold the snow for insulation, yet not to allow too much weight and cave in. Most of the trees for his house he'd fell elsewhere, and have the horses drag them up the hill to his broad bench.

He'd keep their presence in this neighborhood as inconspicuous as possible. The trees he'd leave around the cabin would disguise it. He went back to the old camp to fetch Rachel and his gear and horses up to the cabin site.

Going back, Lyman was conscious of the gorgeous country he had picked for his home. It had always been the way it was now, spread vast and green despite winter's coming. It was all so new and fresh that each day, it seemed, he was seeing it for the first time.

The day was already old, the grey of approaching night seeping in fast. Rachel was at work fixing their meal, sensing that Lyman would return soon.

She laughed at his enthusiasm several times during the meal.

"Above the cave, I found a bodacious shelf for a storage. I'll build a little three-sided shanty up there to cache what furs I don't still have buried roundabout. We can keep fresh meat in it, too. No way the critters and the wolves can get at it, and I'll make a ladder for us to get up to it. Froze meat is almost as good as fresh when you bring down a roast and cook it over your own fire. There's almost enough from the grizzly to see us through, but we have to have variety. I can still hunt and see to packing the meat storage. We won't starve, and that's a fact."

"It sounds like a handsome set-up, Mr. Lyman." Rachel smiled, sharing his excitement.

"I'll build us a nice hearth in the back, you'll see. I can't wait to have you see the place, Rachel. Course it doesn't look like much now, but wait till I get the cabin up. I'm going to see to it that you have a private place there too."

"Haven't had much of that in recent years."

"We'd better get some sleep. I don't know if I can, thinking about the cabin. We've got a good day's work ahead. Get the horses and the gear up there first thing, and then I've got to clear for the base logs and start the walls up. Won't be a big place. Easier to heat that way. But big enough we can swing our arms without hittin' one another. Winter'll be here before we know it, and I don't want to get caught nappin'. That's another reason for keeping it small and simple."

"I'll be glad to get away from this place. This was the end of something awful. The end of my dark memories. I think when I get away from here, things will look brighter."

"I guarantee they will, Rachel."

While Lyman went about the business of building the cabin, always watching the sky for the onset of winter, Rachel learned the camp chores needed to help support Lyman at his work. He marveled at her uncanny knack for seeing what had to be done and pitching in and doing it. This relieved him to devote the short hours of daylight to the building. He was quickly ahead of schedule, though he had no notion of winter's schedule – the sky could be preparing to a dump a load of nasty weather on them.

Rachel tended the horses, kept the fire going in the cave for cooking and warmth, and checked over Lyman's belongings, sorting them for either easy accessibility, or storage when they'd be able to move fully into their winter quarters.

Her trapper companion was busy from first light to pitch dark, pausing only to satisfy an appetite made ravenous by his long hours of hard work. Once when she called him to a meal, he told her he was "hungry as a woodpecker with a headache." It pleased her to be doing for a man again, and watching him tie into his meals, and his pleasure in her support of the effort.

He broke up his long hours of cabin-building by going out to "make meat," as he said, to be stored in his cold-box shanty on the ledge above the cabin. He built it as he had explained to her, and fashioned a light sturdy ladder that would lie alongside the cabin when not in use.

To provide variety in their fare, some of the meat she smoked or otherwise cured after the fashion of techniques she'd learned among the Indians, putting it up in jerky, pemmican, and boudins against the day Lyman would no longer be able to range about freely and hunt.

At the cave's mouth the ground lay flat for some distance.

With their moving about the developing cabin's interior, the earth packed hard and flat, forming the floor of their winter home. Lyman scarcely thought beyond the season of coming grass. Yet, what he was building would serve as a proper base for many trapping seasons to come. All the beaver and other fur bearers a man would want to hunt in a lifetime lay within convenient reach of this place.

Still, he planned he'd range far from home with his trapping. It would, in reality, lessen the hazard for Rachel.

Somehow the fates had decreed that he'd found the almost perfect place for his base camp. There was plenty of game for meat, a good river wasn't far and would be running during the driest of years. Above him, his precious mountains rose, and off from the shelf of his homeplace for Rachel, the tree-whiskered land rolled away without end, a true feast for the eye.

The few thoughts he allowed himself in this direction only spurred him to build the place well. She would need everything he could put into the building of it. After he'd returned Rachel to her people, it would always be here for him to come home to.

Slowly the walls rose as Lyman ventured away from the cabin with his horses to fell the great straight pines, lopping off branches and unusable tops, and dragging them in. With angled timbers for a ramp, he began to lay up the wall logs, carefully hewing close-fitting saddle notches in each, to be laid notch-down to prevent the moisture collecting in the cup-like cuts.

Off away from the cabin site on his log-hunting trips, Lyman revelled in the land. Out here, he could get himself up on a hill and see forever until the sky came down in the distance and shut off his view.

He began to stand in awe of Rachel and her growing vitality. More than a liability in his plans, she was fast becoming an asset. Her wounds appeared to be healing nicely, though he never asked to look at the flayed chest flesh and breast. After her first few days of sickness and fever following the attack, Lyman left to her the attending of the fast-healing wounds.

After those first few days of forced intimacy, sharing the buffalo robe until he could arrange her private bedding, and tending her battered, sick body, the man and woman had separated platonically. Lyman forced himself to put away thoughts of her.

They talked briefly, but only about what must be done — daily and for their future welfare. It was just as well, Lyman thought. Readying things for their long months of wintering over took all their energies, and their talk centered mostly on that. Only now and then, in the moments between eating and rolling up for the night, would Rachel talk about her ordeal among the Indians, and the events that brought it all to pass — the death of her husband in the massacre, and the forced separation from her son. Five years had passed, and while the anguish was nonetheless acute, Rachel was better able to deal with it in her heart and in her talks with the attentive trapper without flooding her face with tears.

Jacob Lyman had become her anchor of emotional stability. They both recognized it, understood it, and kept it in perspective. Lyman was not one to take advantage of an emotionally vulnerable woman. Rachel was hardly a woman to allow it. Though they were already sharing a life together, it seemed this period of distance, of polite and personal privacy, was what Rachel needed. In their days of being together, though apart, a warmth grew in her, Lyman observed. They found things to joke about as the time passed, and Lyman began to take delight in bringing out the merry tinkle of her laughter.

Still, he was aware of a hunger in the woman, a yearning. She put him in mind of some small, soft animal in a cage, hunting for a protection she might never find.

Her warmth and closeness to him seemed to grow with the cabin. She knew it was for her that he was going to such great pains, and she tried to compensate by doing her share, and more. Jacob Lyman, she knew, could have made it in the cave alone, fashioning a barricade of fallen logs and chinking them, arranging a door, thus shielding himself from the elements and winter's roving predators. The amenities of the cabin thrusting from the mouth of the cave, she knew, were for her comfort.

"The bears know a thing or three," he told her. "A cave like that'll keep in the heat, and the log sides hold it as well. The fire ought to give us plenty of light, at least up close. I believe we might even be able to make candles from tallow and sinew for a wick. Maybe later on. Bet you didn't find those books of mine in my possibles; I keep 'em bound together in buckskin and though I've read 'em plenty, they're as good as new."

She had wondered at the thick packets in her sorting, but hadn't investigated. Now she looked forward to the long hours of winter, reading before the fire.

Daily the squared-off room projecting from the cave grew, the logs so carefully notched and overlaid as to hardly need chinking. The door was narrow and low to keep in the warmth. They would have to stoop to enter.

Finally the walls were up, the end logs describing the broad, inverted V of Lyman's desired roof pitch.

Together, with many attempts and sweat much despite the growing cold settling on the land, they hoisted the caplogs and purlins into place.

Each of the heavy roof supports was an ordeal, a trial-and-error affair eased a great deal by the horses pulling as she stood at their heads coaxing them gently forward while Lyman guided the timbers up his two-log ramp.

With the ridgepole and purlins in place, the cabin truly took form. From here it was a downhill job, laying a thin-pole covering at right angles to the ridge and roof poles. The overhang projected beyond the cabin walls at front and sides to give them an avenue around the perimeter in the coming snowdrifts. Already Rachel was stacking their supply of winter fuel along both sides.

Lyman figured winter would attack in all its fury any day.

Rachel was standing back admiring the place as Lyman put the last of his things away for the day after hoisting up the roof supports and trusses.

"I'll commence with the roofing poles in the morning," he said. "But you see now how it'll be. It's like I told you it would be the day I came for you after I found this place."

"It'll be snug, Jacob."

Lyman walked to her side to admire the job so far. "I expect it'll hold till comin' grass time," he said. "With all our possibles and fluff-duff in the cave, you can hardly move around. In a day or so, we'll be able to haul some of that out into the cabin."

"What? Possibles? Fluff-duff?"

"All the baggage. That's mountaineer talk."

"You've done a beautiful job, Jacob. It's a grand home."

"Waugh, I don't know. I suppose it'll do. Have to. I could have laid those logs up truer. But, hell, I'm a trapper. I couldn't drive nails in a snowbank."

"You needn't run yourself down on my account, Mr. Lyman. I say it's beautiful, and beautiful it is."

Forgetting himself in this moment of pride in a job well done and in her appreciation of his effort, Lyman threw his arm around the shoulder of the woman at his side. She had become a fine working partner in the project, and he intended nothing more in the gesture than to show it. Rachel didn't shrink from his embrace. Together they stood, looking at their place. With Lyman's arm casually over her shoulder, Rachel slid her hand along his back until her arm circled his waist.

"Thank you, Jacob," she said softly, and though it was a simple statement, Lyman sensed it was loaded with meaning.

"For what?"

"For this, my snug little cabin. It's the nicest thing that's happened to me in years. Maybe ever. I'll make it a fine home for the winter, Jacob. You'll see."

The moment of closeness coaxed out a boldness that Lyman had struggled to keep hidden. "I'd be pleased, if it's all the same to you, Rachel, if you'd make it Jake."

"All right . . . Jake."

He left it there. "I'll be just ahead of the snows, I'm thinking." Still he kept his arm around her, and she still seemed unwilling to draw away. A warmth flowed into him he hadn't known since first dreaming with the injured woman in his arms. But now it was different. Then she was helpless.

"Tomorrow I'll lay on the roof poles and cover them with branches. That'll keep the topside weather out." He was making words to cover his true emotions.

The air around them was still and cold. Lyman felt something mushy and soft as a feather light on his nose. His face was still warm from his earlier exertion if not from this moment of closeness with the woman, and the stuff melted quickly and ran down to his lip for him to taste with his tongue. Damn, he though, sky ice.

He glanced at the woman beside him, her head barely reaching his shoulders. Heavy snowflakes spangled her soft dark hair like jewels.

"We'd best get in the cave and fire up for the night. She's coming. I won't have a bit of extra time for getting the roof up."

Rachel tightened her arm in an extra hug of the big trapper's waist and pulled away without another word, heading through the cabin walls to the cave. He stood where he had been, watching winter come at last.

When he glanced toward the cabin she was in the doorway, looking back at him, smiling.

Chapter Four

In the long weeks that followed, winter raged in at first like a lion around Lyman's cabin. He had been able to get the cabin roofed over before the major wind squalls and snow blizzards set in. Within a week, the rectangle of logs and the geometric low angle of roof were buried under a soft-mounded pillow of white. Drifts piled nearly to the eaves. The winds were only intermittent; most of the time the land lay locked in the stillness of quiet and bitter cold. It would be a long, hard winter.

All that broke the monotony of rolling fields of snow below the bench where his cabin perched were the pines, standing like silent, cone-shaped ghosts under shrouds of white fur.

The unrelenting grip of winter during that robe season was unseasonally broken as a series of widely spaced chinooks with their warm, spring-like breezes slithered in, thinning the snow cover and warming the air. It could do little more than to make the winter's confinement briefly tolerable.

Two weeks after the first big blanketing snow, the strange warmth returned, waking Lyman to the patter of thawing snow off the ledge of rock outside the cave, and soft shooshing as the pine needles and thin limbs gave up their support of great mounds of snow.

He had only known one or two other winters in the high country when the chinooks came calling, bringing a false, spring-like quality to the land, allowing a man to move about freely and happily and almost warm. Before they started though, they would be over. But Lyman could at least plan on partly taking the cure for that progressive malaise called cabin fever.

Still on the fringes of sleep, warm and snug in his robe in his sleeping quarters in the cabin, Lyman listened with a drowsy ear to the drips and patter, and the snow sliding off pine branches, and let his mind roam free. He had built Rachel a pair of snowshoes of pliable willow woven and tied with rawhide strips. So far, with the hard weather settling in, she hadn't been able to use them. The brief softening brought by the chinook would give them at least a day or so to get out to move around.

Lyman warmly slid in and out of sleep, partly dreaming, partly thinking, of a pleasant, if brief venture away from the cabin this day to teach her to use the giant, cumbersome laced pads, anticipating her delightful tinkle of laughter at her awkwardness in traveling this way.

He realized he had slept again when through its fuzziness he heard her whispered call. He was also aware that in the twilight of dawn, she was crouching beside his bedroll. His night fire was a dying glow on the hearth across the cave.

"Jacob," she said softly beside him in the cabin's dark, bringing him slowly awake. "I need to be with you."

Until now, Lyman had too much respect for the sufferings of his companion, as well as his own sense of decency, to have suggested sharing the bed. He had known an intense attraction for her almost from the start. And often he had felt her eyes on him, and wondered at the message. He had known women but had not known love. As yet he was unwilling to put that kind of tag on his feelings for Rachel. Still there was no mistaking the yearnings he felt for her, and the feelings of longing to protect and provide for her for the rest of his life. Maybe now he could reveal those desires.

Remembering the heat that had come up in him the night of her wounding, Lyman silently peeled back the warmth of his buffalo robe covering, making room for her. It was time, a time he had known was coming when he thought back to that first night. Feelings surged stronger in him, much stronger than the night he had been forced to lie with her after the grizzly attack.

Now that was past, and the eagerness with which she slid in with him and worked the warmth of the robe back around the two of them assured him that for her, too, the past was at last finished. They lay a long time silently together, arms lightly embracing. The only movement Lyman could sense was Rachel's rapid breathing and the quickened thud of her heart against his chest.

Rachel's velvet nakedness touched him full-length, sending tingles into the far reaches of the fiber of him. The smell of her came to his nostrils, that smell that since time began had driven men to all manner of irrational behavior. Still Lyman remained in control of himself.

"Are you all right?" he whispered in the ear now close to his mouth.

"Don't talk," she said, her breath tickling in the stubble of his cheeks. Her lips brushed his several-day growth of whiskers, exploring his face, tracking his mouth. Her first kiss was a warm, almost shy, but at the same time intense, nibble of his lips. It tasted good to Lyman, and shouted at him for more. She pulled away, pausing, her body tensing again, as though she had changed her mind. Suddenly in passion her mouth opened warm and wide seeking his, taking command of the seduction, consuming his mouth with her need.

His own passions mounting, Lyman had matched the intensity of her new embrace with his arms, feeling with his fingertips the tight strength of her back muscles sloping into the rigid, regular lumps of hard spine. Lyman figured it was better to take what came and not trouble himself with questions that had no answers. Intimately, his warm feet felt hers, chilled from her short walk across the cave into the cabin. Something instinctive made him use his warm ones to take the chill off hers. Her knee came up, the calf of her leg slithering over his thigh. After that first kiss of deep emotion, they lay for a long time without movement, without words, experiencing only the closeness they now shared. Neither spoke. Lyman allowed himself to be cloaked in the feelings of tenderness and love for the woman; in these moments, somehow, she had—at last—become his.

Surrendering to the mounting need Rachel signified, Lyman quickly turned oblivious to time and place. He had been so long away from such thrill that Lyman only swam in a deep, pulsing sea of passion, bobbing in its turbulent waves like a cork.

At length he lay like some lazy animal on the tranquil, soft sand of a beach as the wave-like sensations slowly ebbed through and out of him. The sensations washed over him as he squirmed for more comfort in the warm buffalo robe. In this moment of supreme exhaustion he slept, the softness of the woman over him insulated by the coil of buffalo robe that kept out the chill of the cabin that was everywhere around them.

He had no idea how much time had passed before he was persuaded out of the web of sleep by the aromas associated with parching, grinding and boiling of coffee. He was alone, rolled and tucked into the robe. The smells themselves awoke ravenous appetites of a belly kind, appetites that came strongly after a man has satisfied the basic need, as Lyman had less than an hour before. The blanketing aroma of hot, fresh coffee made his mouth water.

Rachel had a fire going at the back of the cave, its warmth and its light filling that end of their hut. Through slitted eyes from the pleasant bulk of his robe, still flat on his back as Rachel had left him, Lyman watched the morning firelight dance against the dark of the ribbed corduroy rows of roofing poles over his head.

Her voice came softly across the room. "If you sit up, I have coffee for you." Lyman swung himself and the robe around, propping his back against the log wall. He ran his fingers through his thick head of hair to smooth it. He realized he did it for her.

When she came to him with the steaming metal cup, Lyman saw a new tenderness in her eyes, a different depth than he had known before.

Lyman took the cup, warming his chilling palms against it, raising it for a tentative sip to test its heat. After what had happened, there seemed little reason for further reserve or secrecy between them.

"Why, Rachel?" he asked. He met her gaze and he let himself smile a little.

The morning fire now had driven the night chill from the cabin and she was comfortable crouching beside him. Rachel had clothed her nakedness, engulfing herself in the massiveness of his warm capote. She also wore the warm, fur-lined moccasins Lyman had fashioned for her.

When she spoke, her voice was soft, intimate.

"I came to a realization in the night. Edwin was a wonderful man. My first and — I thought — my only love. I hope you understand, Jacob, that I will always love him — always have a place in my heart for what we had together."

Lyman nodded, watching her intently over the cup rim, knowing he didn't need to respond with words.

"Five years is a long time, Jacob. Five years with the Indians changed me. I'm different now. But somehow, inside, I refused to yield to the knowledge that somehow all that hadn't happened. That some day I'd wake up and everything would be the same, with Edwin and Daniel back with me. Those years in between were a nightmare and the only way I could live through them was to believe that somehow, someday, I'd be the person I'd been before.

"These last few weeks, with you, have helped to bring me down easily to reality. You have been so patient, so understanding. I've known for a long time of your love for me. I sensed it the night you came back from finding this place for the cabin. I've been in love before, Jacob. I know the signs as clearly as you know the signs of where the beaver live. You confirmed it the night before you finished the cabin roof."

Lyman smiled, still watching her face, remembering.

"It wasn't quite so easy for me. For a long time, since I've known you, it's been hard to sort out. It all had hardened me. I didn't know if I was capable of ever finding love again. I didn't know that the feelings I had for you were not, after all, simply gratitude for the abundance of kindness and tenderness that you showed in everything you did. I tried to explain it away in my heart that way.

"Over it all, my memory of Edwin was an obstacle. He died loving me and protecting me. That's a hard memory to overcome . . . and young Daniel. . . . As I grew in my love for you, there was always that nagging voice telling me that somehow I was being false, faithless to the memory of their love.

"In the night—last night—I wrestled with the thoughts of how going to you would finally close the book on that chapter of my life, and I could begin anew, with you. You so helped bring me back to the reality that Edwin is dead and that Daniel was taken from me. It only seemed right that you should be the one to help me—in your caring love—to manage that realization. You are my one hope, Jacob. It was a very sordid thought, I confess. But I considered that in giving myself to you, I could use it to persuade you—maybe I wanted to exact a promise—to seek out and bring Daniel home to me. That's what first prompted me. Once I was in your arms, I realized that was not the only reason I was there."

Lyman leaned close to her, brushed his lips against her cheek, and resumed his propped position against the cabin wall, clutching the half-empty coffee cup. "I love you Rachel England," he said, and the ease with which he could say it was, in itself, a relief.

She smiled and now it was a winsome smile. "You see? In things like that you endear yourself. Despite your trade in this wild land, Jacob Lyman, you are a gentle man. In things like that you have made me a woman again. Made me a whole person. I love you, too, Jacob Lyman. I will never turn my back on our love."

Lyman turned serious with her words, spoken almost as a vow. He reached out with a free hand and laid his palm over the back of hers, resting close to his.

"There is still that unfinished business," he said.

This confused her and a troubled cloud flitted over her face, her eyes questioning.

"Daniel . . . your son."

"In spite of my cheap thoughts last night, I don't allow myself the luxury of thinking that some day I might find him again, that he might be back with me."

"Don't close your mind to the possibility. Though your life with the Indians was hard, they didn't kill you. They may make virtual slaves of white prisoners, but rarely do they kill them outright unless they are avowed enemies. These five years may have been extremely difficult for your son. But I have a strong feeling that he's alive, somewhere."

Rachel gasped. "Jacob, I hadn't dared hope. Oh, I've had such mixed feelings."

"I can't offer hope. Really. I have thought, come spring, of taking you back east, to be with your people. My friends in this country are spread over miles. Many of them live with Indians. They talk, pass the word of white captives. Not much escapes their attention. And they report. It's going to take a while, probably, but I'll get the word out that I'm looking for information. If Daniel is alive, I can find some trace of him."

"Oh, Jacob, you do offer hope. So much hope."

"But I make no promises. You'll have to be prepared that I may come up empty-handed or with distressing news."

Her eyes clouded. But then she blinked and her chin came up with resolve. Lyman felt a shudder of love. She had guts.

"It's the not knowing, either way, that distresses and destroys."

"Then I'll set out to learn something in the spring. It won't be easy, nor will it be quick. But I swear on my love for you, Rachel England, that if Daniel lives, I'll find him."

"And I want to be here, waiting."

"Rachel, I think not. You'd be better waiting back east, with cultured people. Not out here. I'm gone long weeks, months at a time. I can't leave you alone. And I can't take you with me. That life is much too hard."

"Jake, I have no notion of being out there with you. I'd be a care, just one more thing for you to have to look after. Don't sell me short, Mr. Jacob Lyman. If I thought that some day you'd bring me word of Daniel, or, God permitting, bring him home to me, I could pass the time standing on my head."

"This is a remote place, hard to find. You're safe here. Loneliness is about your only enemy. I could see that you're stocked with meat, everything you need."

There was a very evident eagerness in Rachel now. "And I can take care of things here. Have things ready for you when you get back, and help you before you go. Oh, Jacob, I want it that way!"

Lyman studied on it, but not for long. It would be risky, but then everything in life had its risk. In the months ahead he could instruct her, teach her to shoot. There was that old smooth-bore fusil in his things. He could leave that with her.

She could learn to defend herself, and to make meat if she needed. He could plan his trips, change his style, so he wouldn't really have to be away that long.

The attraction of having her close, waiting for him at home, was strong. Between, them, they could work it out.

"I still don't know," he said. "You'd be safer back east. With your people. I want you to be absolutely sure, Rachel. You're facing long periods of loneliness. But we'll have our winters together—like this. And except for rendezvous, I'll be here with you most of the summers."

She clutched his arm. "Our times together will be good, Jacob. We'll make them that way. What time we're apart, we'll make up for when we're together."

"I just want you to be sure you wouldn't feel safer if you were at home."

Rachel looked at him intently. "This is home."

Impulsively, Lyman propelled himself into her eager arms.

Chapter Five

Making his last beaver set of the day, Lyman sensed his thoughts tending to wander. A man trapping alone has an abundance of time for his mind to play strange tricks, he thought. It was twice as lonely when he was away from his woman. Loneliness, he observed, talking to himself silently as he braved the icy pond, was a fickle companion. Loneliness always changed men, some for the better, some for the worse.

Lyman was not certain how he had been changed by the lonely years before Rachel. He wondered if others who had known him since he had come into the vast mountain country viewed his behavior after his long absences as erratic as some of the men of the mountains he knew.

Would even Rachel see a difference in him after these weeks of solitary trapping and he returned once more to her warm, loving arms? Watch it, Lyman, he told himself; don't get yourself started on those kinds of thoughts. That's what really can drive a man to reckless, insensible behavior.

His mind worked on how the country had affected men he knew. Some showed up wild-eyed and dirty, dependent on a jug, quick to anger, and as quick to express that anger with fists, knife or rifle. Some returned to the company of other men sullen, withdrawn and shifty-eyed, moodily protective of themselves and their belongings.

Others turned foolish, reveling in childish things, given to giggling and prattle, spending the hard-earned wealth from the bounty of the beaver streams on infantile geegaws they either clutched to themselves or squandered on worthless camp-following squaws.

Huh! Lyman grunted aloud. Others never returned. The mountains claimed their tax — and it was a usurious one — on the stamina and the manhood that ventured into their solemn and stern territories for the wealth waiting to be claimed in the abundance of furs.

Sometimes Lyman learned of a man's fate; often he never did. Loneliness could drive a man to the madness that spawned carelessness and made him oblivious to danger; death or disabling injury came to such men without warning. Even alert men were claimed by the elements of heat and cold and the treacherous, fast-moving rivers or steep mountainsides that could slide from under a man as swiftly as a rattler's strike.

But some of this lonely breed, many of them, the ones that counted, grew stronger, more dependable, more reliable and self-reliant, as they met the mountain country on its own terms — unpredictable as it was unforgiving — and bested it.

Jake Lyman considered that he would be counted among those.

Wading hip-deep in a beaver pond, the harsh iciness knotted his muscles with paralyzing spasms of cramp and penetrated knife-like to the marrow of his leg-bones, causing him to tremble convulsively. Lyman mused that at least he had survived quite a few years as a student in this stern school the mountains kept. He fought to control the wild trembling of his near-freezing legs, knowing he could not.

His guard always had to be up, always expecting the unexpected, the unpredicted, and the inevitable. That's where he thought other men sometimes slipped and lost, dropping their guard at the very moment danger reared.

Thinking so deeply, Lyman's own guard was down at the precise moment he became aware of a growing mumbled drone he identified as approaching voices. His first instinct cried danger.

Moving quickly, Lyman groped his way up the slime of the bank, sought out his rifle and other belongings and quickly hid them from sight. He questioned his wisdom, but he knew he would be more mobile without them. His eyes darted, looking for a hiding place. He leaped for the low-sprouting branches of a nearby pine and pulled himself carefully and quietly upward to the obscurity of its dense web of limbs and profusion of long, dark-green needles. Here a man might see, but not so readily be seen. His eye caught movement in the bushes below.

Waiting there, perched among the limbs like some flightless bird, his breathing shallow in anticipation of danger, Lyman watched as five men, their mingled voices still coming to him as a bass monotone, trudged up the river bank to the vicinity of his last trap.

Five, and him alone . . . five to one were risky odds in a game of chance or a fight, he thought, the blend of their voices coming to him muted and indistinguishable. Lyman tried to control his rapid breath, hoping not to wheeze or cough. The five stopped near his tree, knotted together on the stream bank.

"He'll have another along here." One voice came clearly, clinching an identity he had suspected. Bulking under a thick, expensive, hooded capote was Thomas Penn. No mistake. Lyman shuddered in a mixed emotion of anger and fear. Real trouble had found him at last.

Suddenly he yearned for his rifle. Weaponless, he was vulnerable as a treed animal if they spied him.

No one knew much about how or why the cultured Englishman had found his way into the West. Penn was a man with a clouded background and what little was known of him was far from savory.

Neither did Penn's four companions enjoy particularly pleasant reputations among the men who roamed the mountains and the beaver streams. He had been told that Thomas Penn would cut a throat—or order it cut—for a pack of beaver plews.

Penn's black man, John, stood apart from the rest. He struggled to keep his grip on the chains of five or six heavy iron traps slung over his shoulder. The weight of them, Lyman observed, was a taxing load even for the strapping Negro.

The stories Lyman had heard around the forts and the campfires was that John was a decent sort of man. It was also rumored that Penn had bought the black man out of slavery in the South and allowed him a sort of controlled freedom.

"We gonna take this one, too, Thomas?"

Lyman identified the speaker as Simms—he'd run with Penn for years, doing much of his dirty work. Lyman knew of this Simms, and had seen him several times at the posts and along the rivers. Tall and lanky, Simms owned dark and shifty eyes. His eyelids drooped and the grey pouches beneath them marked him as a wasted, dissipated man.

Simms' front teeth, top and bottom, had been knocked out, leaving him with an annoying, lispy speech. When he spoke, his moist, pink tongue darted and licked around the hole in his teeth, giving him a disarming look of stupidity. Stupid Simms was not; treacherous he was.

The only one concerned over the whereabouts of the owner of the trap was the Frenchman, Labelle, who studied the area with darting eyes and swiveling head. Lyman knew that Labelle shared about equal footing in Penn's hierarchy with Simms. As Lyman watched, the stocky Frenchman, who might be a half-breed or quarter-breed, turned, his eyes roving the tall trees. Lyman hunched in fear, trying to hide by making himself smaller. If Thomas Penn's band was caught in this forbidden act of lifting a man's traps, Labelle was prepared to kill to destroy all evidence of their crime.

Labelle's presence spelled another form of threat to Lyman. Good with a gun or a knife, Labelle was even more proficient at killing with the power of his hands and arms, and the enormous strength of his body. He could, it was said, lift his own weight and carry it, and could break bones with his wrestler's hug.

While Simms may have been Penn's confidant, Labelle was Penn's killer and beater of men. A born follower, Labelle willingly owed allegiance only to Thomas Penn. Labelle, though capable of killing with deadly effect, waited for Thomas Penn to tell him who to kill.

Lyman shifted his weight cautiously over the slender limbs supporting him, easing muscles still cramping from the pond's chill, and his awkward position. If Labelle, fifteen feet below and a good twenty-five yards away, was aware of the movement, his actions did not indicate it. Lyman's skin prickled as Labelle turned back to the four at the river's edge.

"This is probably his last one," Penn said. "A man doesn't handle more than six or eight sets at a time. How many have we found?"

Simms glanced at the load on John's back. "John's carryin' six. This one's seven."

A spurt of indignation seared through Lyman. The traps John had slung from his shoulders were his! The Penn tribe had been methodically going along the river destroying his precious beaver sets, stealing his costly traps and bidding fair to putting him out of business as a trapper.

"I doubt we've missed any," Penn said. The man's English was impeccable. It was said he had been well-educated. Lyman could never imagine what had turned Thomas Penn into one of the most loathsome men in the western mountain country.

40

"Get it, Possum," Penn commanded of the Indian standing near him.

"So that's Possum," Lyman thought. He had also heard of Penn's Indian but had never seen him. One couldn't tell his tribal affiliation from his outfit, a ragtag mixture of white man's clothing and Indian buckskins. His hair-style was covered under a battered, round-crowned, flat-brimmed hat. Possum's expression, as well as his posture, suggested stoicism and long-suffering.

Among the men of the mountains, little was known about the Indian. Possum was said to be stupid, or at best very dependent. Despite this, and his stoic expression, he was a tall, virile, and handsome aborigine. Like the black man, John, Possum was one of Penn's two-legged pack animals and the gang's camp tender, a role he held in return for the protection and food of Penn's crew.

From Lyman's cold perch, he watched Possum study his domineering leader with smoldering eyes. Possum clearly had been ordered into the icy water to retrieve Lyman's other traps; his expression suggested that it might be someone else's turn to do the bitterly cold work.

"Get it, Possum," Thomas Penn repeated, sounding impatient.

Possum hesitated, words forming on his lips and escaping in a muttered grumble of Indian words.

"Is that insolence I hear?!" Penn said, his voice rising. "I said, get the trap!"

About to say more, Possum hesitated but a second, gave it up and slid down the muddy pond bank to ease into frigid water well above his knees. He bent low, immersing his arms and chest in the iciness. With a stick, Possum disarmed the cocked trap jaws, their click muffled by the water's depth. Reefing on the chain, Possum pulled the angled wood stake out of the bottom silt where Lyman had prodded it.

Lyman gritted his teeth in fury and frustration at witnessing the theft of his precious traps. He was powerless; any action on his part would be sheer folly. His head trembled in anger as the blood of silent outrage pounded through it. His chance must come to even the tally for this affront. Possum groped his way out of the water, hunched over and shivering, clutching the dripping trap, thoroughly soaked. Lyman might otherwise had sympathized with the Indian's discomfort. He had climbed out of that water minutes before. Possum wordlessly handed the sprung trap for John to add to his already burdensome load.

The black man shifted the weight to ease cramps and the bite of the chains against his shoulders. Hunched and trembling, Possum watched John with compassionate eyes. "Wrong to take these," John spoke up boldly and even loudly. "This is a man's life we stealin'. His work."

Penn drew himself up haughtily. "What is it with you two?! I grant that water's cold and that load is heavy. That doesn't give either of you call to question my authority! So, settle down!" A broad smile crossed Penn's face. "We'll be back in camp soon and we'll warm up around a good fire and pass the jug. You'll forget all about cold water and heavy traps!"

"Who you suppose them traps belong to?" Simms asked.

"Grattan's up here someplace," Penn said. "He'll be no trouble."

"Ly-man?" Labelle asked, and the man in the tree came alert.

"Griz Killer." Penn scoffed. "He's tough, but no match for us."

For a moment, Lyman's anger cooled, hearing the nickname that had spread as his feat was embroidered and elaborated on by the tale-spinners around the trappers' night fires. His thoughts turned to Rachel. Treed by deadly circumstance and trembling with cold, he built a picture of her waiting for him at the snug cabin a week's trip to the northwest. The purplish welts left by the grizzly's swiping claws were the only disfigurement of a beautiful, loving, and vital female body.

Lyman's thoughts were abruptly bounced back to the here and now by Simms' voice, a thin, reedy and whiny kind of sound.

"I'll say this for Griz Killer Lyman. You can be sure when he finds out about this — and he will first thing in the mornin' — he ain't one to knuckle under and run back to the fort, tail 'tween his legs."

"Grattan would if it is him," Labelle said.

"I got a sneaky hunch it's Lyman, Frenchie," John said. "These have been right proper sets we been lifting. A good trapper done 'em. Lyman's a better man, better trapper'n Grattan."

Simms nodded. "He's right. MacLaren, they say, gives prime dollar for a Lyman plew. Or that Lamartine that Griz Killer used to run with. They learnt from the Crows, who can dry a pelt about as good as anybody."

"Look who's in love with Lyman," Penn said sarcastically. "Lyman's got his weak points, and don't you forget it."

Simms and Labelle studied Thomas Penn.

"He's honest and he's proud," Penn said. "He is not sneaky. Any of the rest of them find out about this and you might be afraid of them ambushing us, or creeping into camp in the night and opening a few throats. Not Lyman. He'll come right out in the open about it."

"And they ain't a hell of a lot he's going to do against the five of us," Simms said, a gloating chuckle in his voice.

"Quite right, Simms. Grattan will turn tail, but Griz Killer Lyman would take us all on at once. I know the man, or the type. Matter of honor with them. He'll die, if necessary, to maintain that. And that makes him as much a fool as a coward. More perhaps. Either way, the rest of the beaver in this stream belong to us. And from the looks of things, our Mr. Lyman or Grattan had himself set for some very rich pickings. This is a good beaver country and this is good beaver water."

"Right there's the slide where the beaver been goin' in and out, Thomas," Simms said. "Reckon we oughtta fix it so the beaver won't come out for three, four days like we done them other places?"

"Of course," Penn said. "Labelle, are you ready to do it again?"

Labelle chuckled evilly, fumbling with the front of his buckskin breeches. "Only if I get whiskey to replace it."

"You'll get whiskey, old man," Penn said. "Back at camp."

Labelle stepped to the pond's edge where a groove in the bank mud was worn into a slimy chute for the beaver to return to the water. Labelle spread his feet with his back to the others and noisily urinated on the spot. The foul human odor would spook the beaver for days, possibly weeks.

In spite of the respect for his danger, Jacob Lyman shuddered in a new spasm of fury; he would have given anything right now for his rifle so he could put a big .60 caliber ball into the French breed—integrity and danger be damned! Destroying a man's set and stealing his traps was the most criminal act in this country, short of stabbing him in the back. Labelle's act was the cruelest, most despicable of all.

Probably, Lyman thought, his controlled anger straining to burst out of him in violent revenge, they had similarly spoiled his chances at all the other ponds and dead-water spots along this river where he had made his sets.

He would even the tally for this string of insults, and probably about in the way Thomas Penn predicted. He knew the trapper, George Grattan, the Penn crew had spoken of, but had seen no trace of him in this part of the country. Lyman was sure he was alone, except for these five he had suddenly found himself pitted against.

"Is last trap, Thomas," Labelle said. "Dark by time we get to camp. Whiskey time."

"And time to wait for the appearance of our Mr. Grattan or Mr. Lyman," Penn said.

"I 'ave feeling in bones Monsieur Ly-man is watching us," Labelle said. The others came instantly alert.

"Nonsense," Thomas Penn said. "He's long gone to his camp, wherever that is, skinning out today's catch. His base could be miles from here." The others relaxed. "Come," Penn commanded. "Our work is done."

Lyman watched them go, disappearing into the clumps of aspen and birch with his traps.

Chapter Six

For a half hour after silence returned to the stream bank in the wake of his enemies' departure, Lyman crouched among the thick tree limbs. Penn's words might have been a trick. Away from this spot, Penn might quietly have sent back Labelle or Possum to wait in ambush.

Certain he would have heard anyone returning long before, Lyman painfully eased muscles cramped by his awkward perch and climbed out of the tree. Silently he retrieved his rifle and pouch and stepped to the stream bank where they had stood—to reaffirm his vow of revenge. Even his weak human nose could detect the acrid scent of Labelle's urine. He fought down the fiery urge to move out after them blindly, knowing full well that acting impulsively would produce little more than his own death warrant.

His horses, one for himself and another for his gear, his buffalo robe and other camp comforts, were downstream somewhere in the vicinity of the Penn camp, still hidden from prying eyes. A seasoned man learned to take such precautions. They were hobbled to prevent their straying, but to allow limited grazing. "Better to count ribs than tracks," was the way his old one-legged mountaineer friend, Nate Chapman, put it.

This night Lyman vowed to make a cold camp, think through a plan of attack, and move at daybreak.

Away from the stream, feeling the coming cold of night piercing his clothing, transmitting the chill to his skin, Lyman hunkered down by a large tree, seeking what warmth he could find. He tried to collect his thoughts against his fury and the chaos it caused in his mind. He would not sleep; it would take most of the night to rid his brain of the poison of the outrage and think things through clearly.

Thomas Penn was here purposely to drive him out, to take over his rich streams. Lyman's own set of values dictated that he confront them for this breach of his first-come rights. To do anything less, and especially to turn tail and run, would brand him — certainly in his own mind — a worthless coward. He might as well, then and there, turn his back on Rachel and the cabin and his life and all he held dear in this forbidding country. He would have no life any longer in the West. He might as well return east to the flatlands and the suffocating, humdrum shop existence he had so eagerly and happily forsaken years before to take up this new life, wild and free and danger-fraught as it was.

Lyman's mind burned on a phrase he had once read. "Death before dishonor." It had been etched on somebody's powder horn. To be turned away from the challenge hurled at him by Thomas Penn's coarse insults would be dishonoring himself and all he held to be true.

"Death before dishonor, eh?" he grunted to himself. "There'll be neither!"

Dawn's soft light still carried the bitter chill that had spent the night uncomfortably inside Lyman's clothing. His teeth chattered and he couldn't control the trembling in his joints. He danced and flapped his arms around himself vigorously, feeling warmth driving the cold and stiffness from bones and muscles.

Normally, after a warm, restful night snug in his buffalo

robe, Lyman relished the dawn, particularly if he were on the move, checking for good news in his traps.

An edge of anxiety was in him this morning as he roused himself and moved on without worrying about food. Better to settle this on an empty stomach. More alert that way, he thought. Later, when his mind was at ease, he'd take the time to fix a good and warm meal.

Even the trees stood stiffly as dawn's cold light came up. Lyman edged away from the river, sensing it would be warmer up there, climbing the steep and trackless banks, keeping in the cover of trees, always moving in the direction he knew Penn's camp to be.

Once there, he was not long in finding it. Someone, possibly Possum, was chopping wood, the hollow, rhythmic thunks carrying easily through the trees on the cold, still air. The distinctive mellow smoke from their morning fire grew strong in his nostrils, gripping his stomach with hunger; smells of cooking meat came to him with the smoke. Its vapors were also visible, low-hanging, and clutched between the trees like fog. Thomas Penn was taking absolutely no steps to mask his whereabouts.

Lyman approached the clearing of their campsite carefully. Leaving himself plenty of cover of trees, he edged to a clear view of their camp. With John and Possum busy with camp chores, Penn, Simms, and Labelle were three humped mounds of bulky buffalo robes close to the fire, eating and talking quietly.

A small herd of horses, about eight, grazed at the far edge of the clearing. Lyman sighed in relief at seeing neither of his horses in the bunch; that would be sure indication that Penn had found Lyman's camp.

So far about all they had was his traps, but he had steeled himself that this was an insult he could not, and would not, tolerate. From his secure cover, he hailed the camp. "Thomas Penn!"

The three mounds of buffalo robes circling the fire stiffened. Possum and John dropped what they were doing and edged closer to the trio at the fire. All five were alert, their attention focused in the direction of Lyman's voice. He was well hidden from their sight by the trees.

"Grattan? Is that you, George Grattan?" Penn called.

"You had it right upriver yesterday evening," Lyman yelled. "When you stole my last trap. I was so close I could have shaved you!"

"Marvelous!" Penn enthused, relishing the confrontation with a worthy adversary. "Jacob Lyman! I knew it was you all along. Come in. We'll talk . . . and smoke."

"Smoke! With you? After what you did? And Labelle . . . I should smoke all of you from here with this Hawken rifle. And you know I can do it."

"And have it known up and down the land that you killed from ambush? I rather think not, Jacob Lyman."

"I will have my traps back, Thomas Penn. That and your apology. I won't trouble you more than that if I don't see you again in this territory."

"You're suggesting we leave." It was more statement than question.

"Not suggesting — ordering. Your man Labelle has spoiled these waters for beaver but I will wait that out, provided you leave — at once."

So far none of the men moved from their positions by the fire. Penn, Simms, and Labelle stayed shrouded in their buffalo robes, but now their heads were exposed, the robes in place as capes around their shoulders.

"Jacob, my throat grows hoarse with this shouting. Come in and we'll talk. We mean you no harm. See? Our rifles lean yonder against that tree."

True to Penn's word, Lyman counted five rifles in plain sight and out of their reach. He could easily shoot any man who made a move for them. Lyman paused, considering. He would have to stand here all day bellering his lungs out across the fifty yards that separated them. That would accomplish little. Penn's shout knifed into his thoughts.

"Jacob! A great many lies are spread about me and my men here, all of them grossly untrue. I am not an unreasonable man, Jacob, despite the rumors around the forts."

"You talk of reason. You have destroyed my sets, stolen my traps, fouled my streams. That is beyond unreasonable, Thomas Penn."

"But it achieves my objective. You see? You are here. I needed to talk with you, negotiate with you the purchase of your rights to the fur in these streams."

"There were other ways to find me. And my rights, as you call them, are not for sale."

"Jacob, be sensible. Come in and talk. All this shouting avails nothing. There is more than enough fur here than can be reaped by one man. My four men can take out a fortune before snow flies. I am prepared to reward you amply for that right. You will be well paid, conclude the season several weeks early, and return to your quarters and your beautiful lady."

He knows about that too, Lyman thought, his mind picturing Rachel, and the snug, low-roofed dugout with the thick, gray grizzly robe on the floor before the fire.

With a pang of homesickness out of context with the tense situation, his mind swam with the memory of the cabin's warmth . . . the firelight dancing off the silvertipped fur as he lay with her of evenings, quietly and lightly embracing, entranced by the fire's dance in the dark . . . gently wrestling, giggling wordlessly as their playful passions mounted to a peak.

There was that loneliness again, he thought, and the dangers it can carve for a man.

Lyman pondered Penn's offer. It might amount to a good compromise. The vision of Rachel waiting was compelling. Penn, slimy as he was, provided Lyman a way out without killing or being killed. Penn might be talking straight for once. There would be no dishonor in returning home with gold in his pouch. And he would not have to bargain with scheming traders at the fort for his packs of beaver furs, though he still had stacks cached at various places downstream on his way back to the cabin and Rachel. He made a quick judgement—move in for a parley but stay alert.

"Sit where you are, Thomas. I am coming in. Make no move for those rifles. The first to do that won't live to see the noonday sun."

The three huddled around the now-waning fire held their positions. With John and Possum still standing close by the three, they watched as Lyman came into view through the trees and stepped toward them across the clearing, his rifle down, but ready to be brought up swiftly.

As Lyman approached them, Penn stood, the buffalo robe falling away from his shoulders. His right hand came up with a cocked horse pistol. Simms and Labelle twisted in their seated positions to face Lyman. As they did, their hands too, darted from under the robes with pistol hammers at full cock.

Many yards from them, but exposed in the clearing, Lyman stopped, rigid with shock and outrage at having again been taken for the fool—his traps brazenly stolen and now this.

"The rifle, Jacob," Penn commanded. "Drop it. We have you checkmated."

Lyman's palm sweated around the rifle's forestock, balancing the gun easily ahead of the lock. "Not on your life!" He said it softly.

"Jacob, I have told you I am a reasonable man. Now, do as I say and drop the rifle and there will be no more trouble. Do you think if I had wanted to kill you, I could not have sent Possum or Labelle ahead to kill you at any time. Believe me, Jacob, I am being very generous in allowing you to keep your hair."

Lyman stiffened again. Thomas Penn setting himself up like God Almighty himself in granting Lyman his life. Not only had Penn heaped upon him the lowest form of insult possible in this territory, but Penn had drawn him in with false promises. And then he dared to talk of graciously sparing Lyman's life.

He had risen to their lure like a beaver drawn to a medicine stick suspended invitingly over open trap jaws. Lyman felt a twinge of anger over his own stupidity. But that was secondary to the mound of insult heaped upon him by Thomas Penn by thinking Jacob Lyman so stupid. Lyman was careful not to let his anger goad him into rash action.

"The rifle, Jacob."

Lyman stood his ground and kept his posture of readiness, still keeping his right arm relaxed as he held the big-bore rifle. Without consciously noting that about thirty-five yards separated him from the three armed men, he knew the range to be risky for the short-barreled pistols.

"If you dare to take aim on me with that, you are a dead man, Thomas Penn!"

"Drop the rifle, Jacob!"

"Never, damn you!" Lyman screamed, starting to haul the huge Hawken to his shoulder.

Simms, his flint pistol resting across his left arm, sprung the trigger. As Lyman raised his rifle, he saw Simms' priming powder plume upward with ignition and the enormous puff of smoke as the gun discharged. At the same moment he heard the roar of Simms' giant horse pistol, his left upper arm was torn by some monstrous force, jerking him rudely off balance. His right arm came up and he dropped the Hawken to clutch involuntarily at the wounded arm. He was not aware of having been hit by Simms' pistol ball; his first sensation was that he had been struck by lightning.

Though the ball had only passed through the flesh of his arm, he twisted with the shock of the bullet's force and dropped to his knees in agony. In an instant, he recovered his senses and his right hand groped for the dropped rifle in the blind need for survival.

With the shot, Labelle had leaped up and was on him, a powerful knee coming up to catch Lyman under the chin with a resounding crack that sent him sprawling away from the rifle. Labelle eased down the hammer of his piece, shoved it into his belt and stepped to Lyman, pulling him rudely to his feet. Lyman's consciousness was alive with darting arrows of brilliant light from the viciousness of Labelle's kick and the agony of his shoulder and arm. He did not fully comprehend what was happening.

"Up, mon ami, up!" Labelle growled, getting behind Lyman and pinning his arms. A new sear of pain drenched the shattered muscles. Through eyes dimmed by his agony, Lyman saw Penn and Simms running toward him and Labelle. Possum and John approached more slowly.

Feeling and smelling Labelle's sour breath panting on his neck, Lyman sensed a crazy, panicked fright rising in him and he jerked and squirmed in a sudden spasm of wild strength. Death was close and he fought to escape it with superhuman effort. Still, Labelle's iron grip resisted him firmly and painfully.

Simms had replaced his discharged pistol with a loaded rifle from the stack at the tree. Thomas Penn came up with rage printed on his face. "Simms! That fool threatened my life!"

"I know, Thomas, I know," Simms said, handing the rifle to Penn. He stepped in front of the restrained trapper and cocked his arm to drive a sledgehammer fist into Lyman's midriff below the breastbone. Lyman nearly blacked out again as the force drove the wind from his lungs in a giant grunt and replaced it with a suffocating paralysis. Pinned as he was by Labelle, Lyman regained a brief equilibrium. With Labelle supporting him, he brought up both legs and lashed them out, kicking Simms away, connecting solidly with the rangy cut-throat at gut level. Fully enraged, Simms caught himself and waded back in at Lyman, still held firmly by Labelle's iron grip. Penn stood beside Simms, egging him on.

"This here mud duck's askin' to git a lesson learnt him," Simms lisped through the gritted hole in his teeth. Penn nodded and grinned, relishing the battering of Lyman. Simms' knee came up, taking Lyman in the groin, knocking the trapper completely senseless. His head sagged.

Simms hoisted Lyman's head by the hair, hauled back his arm and drove a punch straight into Lyman's mouth. His lips split, spewing blood over his face and down the front of his buckskin shirt. Lyman was insensitive to the blow. Simms jabbed Lyman's cheekbone, following through with another flailing fist into Lyman's right eye.

"Give him it, Seems!" Labelle hissed in encouragement past Lyman's ear.

"Stop it!" A screamed shout caused Simms to pause in cocking his arm for another blow. In astonishment, Labelle loosened his grip but did not lose it. Lyman was only vaguely aware of the action.

At Penn's and Simms' backs, John had a rifle cocked and levelled at the group.

"You done give that man enough," John said, a new authority in a voice accustomed to fawning. Penn and Simms whirled to face the black man. Thinking quickly, Thomas Penn tossed the armed rifle at Simms, who caught it with a deft catch.

"John! Don't be a fool!" Penn yelled, bringing up his loaded pistol.

"Mister Penn, I been a fool enough years! Time I stood up to your beatin' and cheatin' helpless men!" John shouted with angry passion. "Drop him, Labelle!"

Possum stood off from the tight cluster of men, watching John intently.

"Drop him, I said!" John repeated. "Step away. This gun's aimed straight at Penn!"

"Do it!" Penn screamed. John had made a desperate bid for freedom and Penn sensed the man was determined enough not to hesitate in carrying out his threat. "That nigger's gone totally mad!"

Lyman landed at the feet of Simms and Penn as Labelle stood, disbelieving, arms out at his sides. John quickly stepped to Lyman's side, angrily bumping Labelle out of the way. Keeping the rifle in the crook of his arm, finger on the trigger and pointed at Penn, John eased down and lifted the groggy Lyman by his good arm.

"Get your gun," he commanded. Lyman slid easily out of John's grip and made his painful way on hands and knees the few feet to retrieve his rifle. Despite the battering and pain, Lyman was aware that the scales had tipped in his favor. He was still unaware why or how the black man had come to his aid. His thoughts slowly became more clear through the haze of pain.

"You'll die for this, John," Penn muttered through teeth gritted in rage. "I gave you every opportunity." Penn levelled his pistol at Lyman and his new ally. Labelle edged to Penn and carefully swung up and cocked his belt pistol. "You fools are dead men," Penn growled, his aristocratic face dark and tight in fury at John's insolence.

Lyman found his voice. "You may get us, but one of us will get you, Thomas," he croaked through split lips.

"Four against two," Penn sneered. "Don't force it, Lyman!"

"When I walked in here, it was five against one. I just doubled my chances." Lyman didn't dare sneak a glance at the black man standing resolutely beside him. He felt his chest swelling with their bond of common purpose. "And only three of you got guns. So let's get started and see who's left standing!" He was conscious of John stiffening in readiness. Lyman yearned to look into John's eyes and to grin in reassurance that he was doing the right thing.

"Possum!" Penn yelled. "Grab a rifle and get up here!"

"He already has it," John declared with ominous tone. Penn dared to crank his head around to see Possum, supposedly blindly loyal, holding his rifle on the three of them, squarely aligning himself with Lyman and John.

"Possum stand with John," he said in a bass voice ominous as a war drum.

"Of all the ungrateful savages and slaves!" Penn shouted impulsively, firing in Possum's general direction. Hit, or dodging the shot, Possum rolled sidewise and landed in a heap. Lyman's attention focused on Penn, who swung around to face him again.

"Shoot!" Penn screamed at Simms and Labelle.

Beside him, Lyman heard the deafening roar of John's big rifle. Over the muzzle blast of smoke he saw Penn slammed off his feet and driven down, flat on his back in the dirt. Penn lay still, blood staining his shirtfront.

Wisely, Lyman saved his single shot, keeping the gun trained on Simms and Labelle. He also kept his stare, now fully alert, on the face of the pair.

"Penn's out of it," Lyman growled. "Now it's up to you. One of you will go down, make no mistake. I shan't miss at this range."

Simms and Labelle wavered, wanting to look back to see how seriously Penn was hurt. They dared not.

"I told you Penn's out of it!" Lyman screamed in a new fury. "Now do something." Past them, he could see Possum coming to his feet, unhurt, and reaching for the rifle dropped when he ducked Penn's shot.

Simms and Labelle continued to stare at Lyman, their expressions registering a panicked awareness of movement behind them. "Thomas?" Simms called anxiously, directing his question out the side of his mouth.

"Huh-uh," Lyman said, and his smugness was evident. "Possum's got his rifle pointed straight at your backs. Now you both will go down."

Labelle darted a look over his shoulder and dropped his pistol. Simms did the same, the fight gone out of the two of them.

Thomas Penn was not dead. The bullet had torn through his shoulder close to his neck. Nearly unconscious with the wound and the shock, Penn writhed in agony on the ground.

A reservoir of new strength pumped power into Jacob Lyman, a vitality spawned by the rescue of his very life by his two new allies, John and Possum. Misery, Lyman recalled, a grin near the surface, loves company. Thank heaven, he thought, for misery. He had been saved by the years of misery the black man and the Indian had endured silently at Thomas Penn's hand.

"There's horses over there," he told the two facing him. "Bundle your boss on one. He isn't bad hurt. He'll live, maybe, till you can get him to a fort. You may each have a riding horse out of the bunch and that's all. Now get along. Tell Penn we're keeping the rest for what he's done—to me and to these two."

"We ain't going to have no supplies, Mr. Lyman," Simms whined, fawning now with fake courtesy, his thin voice sounding like a pouting child. "It's a long ways to the fort with no guns."

"Think about that the next time you take it into your heads to ride into my territory. Maybe then you'll think twice. Because if I ever catch you in these woods or anywhere near where I am, Simms, I'll knock out the rest of those teeth. Labelle, I'll hamstring you!"

Simms glanced at his pistol in the dirt, thought better of it and stepped back to pick up Penn. Labelle joined him, shoulders stooped in humiliation, for the moment totally beaten. Lyman stood his ground as they helped a dazed

Thomas Penn toward the horses. Lyman's body was racked with the agony of his wound and the beating, lessened now by the supreme thrill that he had not only survived, but had triumphed and gained two staunch allies.

"And stay out of my territory!" he called after them. Lyman now dared to glance at John, whose black face was wreathed in a tooth-flashing smile. Lyman added, "I mean stay out of OUR territory!"

His eyes swung on Possum, studying him suspiciously from a distance.

"Come on over here, Possum," Lyman yelled jubilantly. "That means you too!"

Possum's dark and handsome aborigine face was spread with a grin as big as John's. He brought up his rifle to port and marched proudly to take his place beside Lyman and John and watch the defeated trio make ready to ride out of the camp.

"Jacob," Possum said. "Him honorable man!"

Chapter Seven

"Jake, do you think you're fit to go down there and help John and Possum with their cabin?" Rachel hovered over him again this morning, as she had in the days since his return, like a ministering angel.

He flexed his wounded arm, aware of its progressive healing since he had returned to the cabin. Being with Rachel was a healing influence, he thought—to the body as well as to the soul.

"It'll do me good. A man can lay up in a cabin only so long before he starts to tighten up again. I swear that trouncing I took left me with the miseries where I'd never felt 'em before. The trip back was mean on aching bones, too. My toes hurt and so did the roots of my hair, bouncing along on that old mare." Lyman's jokes were only superficial; the trip home had been agony. "I don't particularly look forward to going through anything like that again. Good that I found those two. Between them and you looking after me, I'm about knitted back up to where I ought to be. Lord knows where I'd have been now if it hadn't been for them."

"Jake, don't talk like that. It frightens me. You know you're all I've got."

"And you know that goes both ways."

"John said that awful Penn has an idea where our place is. Would he come here? For revenge?"

That thought had gnawed at him since the brutal confrontation. He had even tried to reassure himself that Penn would never find the cabin and Rachel. It was a big country . . . but then again, Thomas Penn was not noted for being backward when it came to getting even. Lyman told Rachel what he had been trying to tell himself.

"Nah! All campfire talk. The story's traveling fast, about the bear and . . . you. Penn and his cronies have just heard campfire talk."

"I did some shooting while you were gone . . . with the gun." Rachel sounded as though she were changing the subject. But he wasn't so sure her response didn't have to do with the same fears, at least as it concerned her own welfare and protection. "What did you call it?"

"The smoothbore. The little feller. It's a trade gun. Always kept it with my possibles in case anything happened to the big rifle. How'd you do?"

"You were a good teacher, Jake. I've learned to keep a fine sight, to hold my breath, to just squeeze the trigger, and not to jerk before the hammer falls. It's alien to me, but I guess if I'm going to be here with you—and Daniel when you find him—I'll learn to be a mountain man's woman."

"I expect I'll find trace of him or something at rendezvous in the summer. I heard a few stories here and there this trip, but nothing I could sink my teeth into."

"We'll find Daniel, Jake. It's only a matter of time. That hope sustains me. That, and knowing you'll be back."

He looked at her, but put aside thoughts of taking her in his arms. He still felt the glow of homecoming love the night before, the first he had felt up to since his return and his recovery from the battering by Simms and Labelle. Still, Rachel had slept by his side each night.

He looked around him, still marveling at the things that

were new to him that she had managed while he was away. "Well, the place sure looks good. You've made it into snug quarters, Rachel. Warmth around a place is more than fires and thick logs and a roof."

"I wanted it nice for you when you got back. I had to keep busy."

"Seems you did. And glad that you've been working with the old fuzee. Get any meat?"

"No, you left me with more than enough. But I could. Now."

"Good. If the bad weather holds off and I can help John and Possum get their rafters up, we'll get out and you can show me how well you do. There are new rifles and pistols to work with, too. Those I took off Penn. His is a fine one, an expensive Hawken; I imagine he's burning about that. Simms and Labelle's rifles are only middling pieces, but will do in a pinch. John and Possum have them; they insisted I keep Penn's rifle. I want to leave that here with you. We three each now have a pistol of our own; I never had the good fortune to own a pistol. With the smoothbore and Penn's fine rifle, you're well armed. I'll stick with old Griz Killer yonder."

Despite the small talk, their thoughts still hovered around the Penn menace.

"Rachel?"

"Yes?"

"Come. Sit here with me."

Obediently, as though knowing some things needed to be brought into the open, she left her work by the hearth. She perched beside him on the mound of robes that constituted their bed and their chairs. She searched his eyes with hers.

"I love you for what you've done to this place. Your touch is everywhere. You've made it a home for me to come back to."

"Something's on your mind, Mr. Lyman."

"We both know it—Penn. I don't think I can leave you when he knows I have a woman somewhere. Just the sort of trick he'd pull to get even."

"I told you I can take care of myself."

"We've got to face things the way they are, Rachel. I want you to consider going back east."

She stiffened. "Not while there's a shred of chance that Daniel is alive somewhere. And you know I have to be here for you. It's out of the question."

"I just don't think it's fair to put you in so much danger."

"Mr. Lyman! Do you think I'm some child fresh out of some eastern finishing school? I may have been a babe in the woods when I left to come out here. Remember that I survived a massacre, and five years as a slave of the Cheyenne. I've also had almost another year here, much of it alone."

Lyman studied her.

"I can handle myself," she said. "I must say, though, that I'm grateful for the rifle. I'll keep both of them loaded. That ought to discourage just about anyone."

Lyman ignored her talk about the guns. "You could go to rendezvous with me. Mr. MacLaren can take you safely to St. Louis with his mule trains. I'll come next spring with Daniel or with word of him. I'll spend all the time I can trying to find Daniel."

"You're doing that anyway. No, Jacob. I feel more at ease here. This is a big country, you yourself have said it over and over. This is only a small corner of it. I feel safe and secure here and I wouldn't back east. I'd lose my mind fretting about you and Daniel. It just won't work."

"Then I'll stay here and send John and Possum to rendezvous with our goods. They can trade for me, and ask about Daniel."

"Jacob Lyman, you dear man. That won't work. You'd be like a caged animal staying here. I won't stand for that either.

You need to go there, to look after your own affairs. You also need to go there to do whatever is it you do with old friends. You've told me how much you look forward to rendezvous."

"Well, all right. I guess I don't like it, but you are a strong woman, and you sure are wise to the mountain ways." He grinned as it all finally resolved itself in his mind. He guessed he'd worry more if she were in St. Louis.

"There's another reason I have to be here; to be here for you."

"What's that?"

"You are silly," she said. "Of course you have no idea." She reached toward him in a hasty embrace and as they hugged, their lips meeting, she touched, probed and stroked him in seductive ways, in sensitive places. Tingling, Lyman felt his passions mounting.

"But I read the sign," he mumbled through lips touching hers.

"Hello, the cabin!" came a voice from outside. It was John.

"Damn!" Lyman said, pulling away.

"Don't encourage him to stay forever," she whispered, pulling away from Lyman and smoothing her clothing.

Memories of their childlike, carefree loving were strong in Lyman's thoughts two weeks later when the three trappers, their mounts and pack animals crested a ridge miles to the west. Rendezvous was in the air, no mistake of it. It was as yet unseen, unheard and unsmelled. But it was there over a couple more ridges and down into the basin. Already Lyman sensed a heady anticipation in the air around him. In a matter of minutes, they'd spy it, the great lush sprawl of land thronged with lodges, horse herds, trappers, Indians, trade goods and whiskey.

And revelry; mountain men fixing to paw and beller.

Lyman could tell that Possum and John had been champing at the bit to get there for the last hour. He surely had no reason to hold his partners back and yet they tarried almost impatiently as if awaiting his by-your-leave. They were that close now and the eager tension was in the two of them, and in the looks they darted at him.

Lyman grinned. Their first rendezvous free of Penn's shackles. Their first as free trappers. For the first time in their lives, they had plews to trade for whatever benefit they might give. No wonder, he thought, that they were acting like hobbled colts. Nine months with these two; good months since they had allied themselves with him against Penn. Both were good trappers and fine woodsmen. Something unspoken caused them to stick together in the wake of the confrontation with Penn. Lyman happily accepted them as partners, and the unlikely pair grew with the opportunity to share the rewards along with the responsibilities.

The three-way alliance had extended itself to the snug shanty Possum and John had constructed a mile or so from the Lyman digs. He'd even been able to spend some of the spring days helping them with it after he'd recuperated from his wound and beating he'd taken from Penn's hirelings.

"I don't know what the hell you two are waiting for," he said. "Get on down there if you want to. I'll catch up with you."

Whooping like boys out of school, Possum and John put knees to their horses' ribs and were gone in clouds of dust among the scattered trees. Their respective pack horses, backs swollen with thumping, flopping packs of furs, consented to being led at this fast pace, but only reluctantly. Silence and solitude fell upon Lyman in the wake of their leaving. It was good, just as well. He'd been with Possum and John for weeks – months, actually, even during the time of his short trip home. It was good to have these next few minutes alone. To think. The days ahead would be crowded with shinin' times, new doin's, old faces.

The days between rendezvous, in Lyman's scheme of things, simply flowed past like water in a tumbling brook, sometimes bright and chatty, sometimes dark and subdued, depending on the character of the sky overhead and the mood that lay on the land. The beauty was that he was free in all of it; like the river, free to go wherever the spirit moved him.

Yet, the days once gone were out of his grasp, taking a part of him with them—like a twig with a dancing leaf torn off a sycamore floating downstream. Days spent brought age and age could creep up on a man, robbing him of his vigor bit by bit. In this country he had to stay lean and flexible, young and alert. The land demanded it.

At thirty or thereabouts, he still had a lot of years to trap and hunt and rendezvous and love Rachel. In youth, it seemed time had been infinite. With maturity, time took on a new, different and truncated dimension. The day was coming when he'd look ahead and damned near see the end of his days looming out there like a great black cloud. The time between rendezvous marched ahead without reckoning.

Maybe it was because he carried no watch but was regulated by the rhythms of life—sunup, zenith, sundown, empty gut, full gut, drop the britches, squat, grunt, and move on. Time was counted only by the ready-to-burst waxy buds of spring or the crisp, brittle death of fall, the hot noisy thundertorrents of summer, or winter's vast solemn fields of bitter cold and blinding white. When was Thursday, Thanksgiving, a man's thirtieth birthday, his fiftieth, if he made it that far? For men like Jake Lyman, time, or the need of it, seldom existed.

The mountain breed saved up the holidays for just this time ahead, he thought. Christmas and Fourth of July and birthdays and all the rest got packed into ten or so days at rendezvous. Even that, for some of them, wasn't enough. Ten or so days that, once the trading and the settling up was done, a man sucked and drained everything he could from sunup to sunup and around again. There'd be plenty of time for sleep after the plews were spent on vast quantities of

"Touse" whiskey and "awardenty," and the beads and gee-gaws and foofurraw were handed over to roistering Indian girls for a crack at their crotches. Sleep was all you had left after the lodges were struck and packed, the departing travois sending up dust clouds, and the company's mule carts were loaded with the season's furs and pointed east.

In the void of silence that followed, the sadness and the regret would come. And the biggest sleep of all was out there waiting and maybe it would come before rendezvous came around again. So live, love, and laugh for today, for tomorrow, old hoss, we may be gone under.

But Jacob Lyman had other plans. Oh, he knew he'd had his share of shinin' times. This year, things had a new meaning. He had no need of the delicious little mahogany girls in their buckskins bleached white, soft as goosedown, and heavy with quillwork. When they made a suggestive hole with left thumb and forefinger darting the right finger in and out accenting availability, he'd ignore them. His mind turned again to Rachel: Why would a man gnaw jerky when he had tender hump ribs on the fire at home? That was the difference, he thought, between love and lust.

And whiskey. He'd have some; after all it was rendezvous. But he'd nurse his pail of it, having only enough to stay light and mellow.

Filled with resolve, Lyman crested the ridge. His stillness and room to think were replaced with the frenzy and fever and excitement and activity of the annual grand encampment—the old familiar tug of getting to rendezvous strong in him now. Up and down the lush, green valley, lodges slanted skyward against azure grass about as far as the eye could see, seeming to stand clean and somehow new. Already smoke from a hundred campfires hung in rifted tendrils close to the land, pungent and distinctive even at Lyman's vantage point high on the ridge.

Below him in the humanity-filled basin, men were in

motion like bees around pink, spring-fresh clover, marching singly or in clusters or standing but busy gathering in the nectar of the talk, the drink, and the laughter of rendezvous.

These times would have a character all their own that made other times somehow more tolerable.

These were sights to be savored and recorded because the day would come when their memory might be all that would keep a man's mind glued together in the lonesomeness of a vast, silent, and cold land.

Lyman continued to rest on the ridge and let his horse blow, taking inside himself the panorama of rendezvous — lodges pitched helter-skelter below him like precise cones in a geometry book; bright splashes of color in blankets or in calico shirts specially saved for the occasion. Nearer to him herds of horses cropped the perimeter grass, sneezing and whickering, relaxed and content that no demands were being made of them. The sounds, too, swirled around him as he absorbed this first euphoric encounter with rendezvous. Voices and laughter rose up to him like a sigh in a single, steady drone, punctuated by yells, whoops of recognition and welcome, and the occasional crisp, crunching crack of a Hawken rifle fired either at a mark or merely at the dim wafer of daytime moon in a wild frenzy of jubilation.

Already men were crowding and bellying up to the counters set on bales by the *engagees* and clerks of the big fur companies like Alexander MacLaren's Western Fur Company. Make-do counters, perched on bales shaded by jury-rigged awnings, groaned with trade goods and made a traditional place for the commerce of rendezvous. Here, Lyman knew, he'd find the best and the least of necessities to suit mountaineer or Indian; the essentials of his trade for the next year, and the fancies that had no other utility than to purchase poontang. And it looked at though this year's rendezvous would be overstocked with that commodity.

Among the trappers, plews counted for next to nothing with each other, except what they would bring from the traders and the fur companies' stores. So, the business of rendezvous was already progressing at a brisk pace as Lyman urged his horse at a walk down the slope and into the melee below him. As fast as the furs were whisked over the counter and the bargains struck, they were hustled to the rear of the hasty mercantile for baling. There the *engagees*, MacLaren's workmen, pressed the many bundles of plews soon to be bound for St. Louis and ultimately, the felt hat factories of England and the continent.

The soft underfur of winter-prime beaver, fluffy and delicate as new snow, suited marvelously for hat-making, Lyman had been told. This particular kind of hair had fine barbs which interlocked for the craft of hat-making, matted under heat and pressure into thick felt. They called them beaver hats, but to Jake Lyman, there was hardly any similarity.

Lyman threaded his way through the herds of horses with their muzzles bent to the grass of the hillside. The grazing, contented animals, roans and blacks and eye-catching paints, graciously made an avenue for him to pass through, though scarcely acknowledging the man on horseback.

Chapter Eight

Near where Lyman rode down into the flats, the congregated mountain men moved about, talking and drinking and queuing up with some Indians at the counters where MacLaren's men had set the company's goods. The Western Fur Company's clerks and factors stood busily shoulder to shoulder, pulling in the plews, shoving forward the agreed-upon goods, and jotting significant information in their account books. Nearby the *engagees* were equally busy, packing the furs for the return to St. Louis. The hollow, knocking sounds of the driven wedges added to the din of commerce as usual, pressing the hides and furs into convenient but ponderously heavy packs.

Lyman studied the scene for a moment, deep in thought, a mild sensation of depression coming on him again. Rendezvous scarcely begun, and already it was commencing to be over. When the last of the plews had been bargained for, and the last bale toppled out of the huge wooden press, MacLaren and company would be tugging at the tether to get headed east again, and it would be all over.

Oh, the mountain men and the Indians would stay until the last drop was drained from the jugs, and until the last squaw had been bedded for a handful of beads. Still, after the eastbound mule-cart trains of furs left, the heavy silence would gradually seep in. The excitement and the exuberance would wane, the whoops would come less frequently, the shooting would still. Men would sit around quietly talking, reluctant for it to end, and then it was time to say goodbye for another year.

Lyman's spirits sank a bit more. All these weeks and months of backbreaking work and life-threat for this. And it was all over before it really started.

Then his eyes moved from the busy MacLaren store and the men at their jobs of commerce to the revelry that outshined all that. He felt again the quick surge of excitement. Through some blessing or divine intercession, it rarely rained on rendezvous. He couldn't actually remember when it did. This day was perfect for the event, a warm sun glazing everything with a soft yellow, the clouds burned off save for one wind-tattered puff standing starkly alone way to hell and gone down the breathtaking dome of soft blue. As his eyes measured the single cloud, a hawk drifted into view, gracefully and lazily riding the sky on outstretched wings. Below, the river flowed through a row of cottonwoods standing like haphazard sentinels, the grass-covered hills beyond dotted with the horses. The lodges loomed larger now, their straw-thin lodgepole tips extended like fingers waving at the sky, and the smoke lazily rose around and through them. Between the lodges, the mountain men and the Indians moved, enough like brothers to be kin, but distinctly different in manner and dress.

Indian faces were stoic and the color of old brass, framed in the hair styles peculiar to their tribe or nation. The expressions of the white trappers were distinctly different. Out of faces old before their time, ribbed and dark from exposure, their eyes were almost paradoxical, young and bright, searching and alert as birds protecting a nest.

Though he was one of the buckskinned breed, Lyman never quite fit in. Around him now they seemed to be a congregation of strangers as they moved about in their rag-ged, grease-stained buckskins, tatters of ribboned beadwork still showing on some.

Threading his cautious way through these teeming throngs, Lyman felt his ears assaulted by more noise than all the sounds he'd heard in the past twelve months put together. What had been muffled and provocative from the hilltop threatened now to suffocate him in its rising intensity – gun blasts, yapping dogs, screeching Indian kids, the raucous cough of braying jackasses that had hauled in all the trading paraphernalia from out East, exhilarated trappers whooping it up, and the sharp, shrewish voices of old crone-like squaws arguing and scolding in their lodges.

Lyman also know that within minutes, his system and his senses would adjust; then it would seem strange when the quiet returned.

He caught no glimpse of Possum and John and their pack horses loaded with the year's catch. There was still enough time in the day to get their trading done, find a hospitable lodge to cache their new-bought fixin's and get out and get to rendezvousin'!

Still feeling oddly alone in the midst of this madness, Lyman led his horses through the active, noisy camp, his eyes seeking a familiar face or form. Beside him, from a clot of yammering mountaineers, one of them tore himself away, hobbling abruptly toward Lyman.

A great grin split the craggy, whiskered face. "Jaayykk Lymannn!" a voice roared at him, a voice thin with age and weathering. Maybe it was because they talked so seldom, Lyman thought, but mountain men rarely had pleasant voices.

For a second or two, Lyman was hard put to hang a name to the face. It wasn't long in coming. He hadn't seen one-legged Nathan Chapman in two seasons.

"Howdy, Nate," Lyman said with a thin smile of recogni-tion. What his salutation lacked in matching exuberance, it made up for in sincerity. With Chapman's guffaw of greeting, he rushed up and socked Lyman's shoulder familiarly with his fist.

"Damn, Jake, ye con-demned idjit, you're a gentle sight for these sick old eyes."

"Missed you last year, Nate."

"Right as rain. I was, you might say, otherwise engaged. Wintered and summered up in the Absaroky country, I did. I've wived again, Jake, and it's made me chipper as a coopfull of catbirds. Taken me a fine little Crow woman. Pleasant soul, she is, a right prime possible for this old bone. Onliest English she knows is yes, and that only to me. And she sure does shine at fixin' for a man. Me, I couldn't talk Crow to a blackbird, but we get by, her and me. Good arrangement. I bring home the meat and the hides, and Dawn Calf cures, cooks and jerks the meat. Puts up as fine a set of mockersins as you'll shove a hoof into."

"She here?"

"Right as rain. Lodge is down yander. Dawn Calf is there now, roasting some hump ribs and dicin' and grindin' and stuffin' for tonight's boudins. Say what you want, but the hivernant don't grow that can shine to a Crow for slick. Make the peartest, by God, fixin's and skins ye'll put on your back, and they ain't a lodge made that shines to a Crow's for handsome. Crow beaver'll find favor over yer reg'lar Missourah plews put up by a mountaineer at ary rendezvous. Alexander MacLaren here, he'll give extry measure of beads an' foofurraw to git Crow beaver and fur, I'm here to tell ye. Well, you know, Jake, you an' Rene Lamartine must've learnt from the Crows. They say they ain't a better plew than what's put up by you, or old Lamartine when the two of ye . . . Well, find you some 'Touse' to fill my can, Jake, and I'll be obliged to have you by when the meat's done."

"I expect I'd look kindly on that, Nate. Got to find my pardners directly."

"Pardners? Who you paired up with these days, Jake? You was always solitaire, except for that one season with Lamartine." A cloud seemed to slide over Nate's expression, his eyes thoughtful. "Oh, I got to tell you something about Rene, but now ain't the time. Who you been pardnerin' with?"

"You'll never believe."

"These old ears has heard some strange ones. Tell me."

"You recollect an Indian name of Possum and a black man they used to call Nigger John?"

"Why, Jake, they's Penn's men! Here, wait up! You ain't tied up with that heathen, have ya? Ol' Penn's about as worthless as a four-card flush, a high-falutin' primee-donny in hellaciousness. Weasel blood in him, they is. That Possum, he a Crow? Crows is magnificent thieves, ye know. By God, I calc'late them con-demned idjits could steal the hump meat off the tip of your Green River knife between the fire and your yap! They're that slick."

"Wagh, Nate," Lyman said in exclamation. "More like a couple of Penn's boys tied up with this heathen." He told the old mountaineer of the trap theft, his confrontation with Penn, and of Possum's and John's sudden switch in allegiance as they walked. That seemed to be enough for the moment. In his good time, he'd talk with Nate of the months between with Possum and John and of the fact that he, too, now had a woman. Sometimes it worked better for a man not to unload his guts all at once.

Nathan Chapman wasn't much of a hand to listen too long in one spell as it was. Some men just couldn't take too much of a monologue before losing attention and wanting themselves to get at something that was festering in their minds and they'd have to get it out. And Nate did.

"You talk of that Penn. Now, I seen that con-demned idjit jes' the once. I didn't need more. I don't shine to his lingo. He spouts words that run about eight to the pound. Everybody knows the way his stick floats. I told the son of a bitch that

73

when he was dead I wanted to know where he was buried bein' as I calc'lated to honor the dead by plantin' a bull thistle over his burying place. I allowed as to how I'd come by regular and water it with corn squeezin's once removed. I told him they'd never have to worry about the grass growin' where he was put under. All his bullshit'd keep the land around green for nigh a hunderd years.

"Hell, Jake, if I bought and paid for ten teams of ornery jackasses and got Penn, I'd be overstocked!"

Lyman chuckled.

"Come on," Chapman said, "walk down to my lodge and see little Dawn Calf. Get a load off them hosses. They commencin' to look plumb gant with them packs of furs. From the looks of things, you had you a good season. You can turn your hosses out with my string."

"Could I cache my possibles in with your woman to look after?"

"Right as rain. Be proud to have you. You can spread your robes in with me too, if you like, Jake. Some just sleep out, but me I get partial to my robes under cover of the lodge in my old age. 'Special a Crow lodge."

Together they moved away from the noisy tables of commerce and into the rendezvous camp proper. Before one lodge a dozen trappers clustered and crouched, gambling at the game of hand. Near them, a bright-eyed and expectant mountain of a man in buckskins was bargaining, showing a bright-red bolt of cloth to a wisp of an Indian girl not a day over thirteen. Lyman couldn't hear the conversation, but the girl smiled, shyly averting her eyes and taking the rectangular wad of cloth. Together the two trudged off in the direction of the fringe of cottonwoods skirting the river to consummate the Indian girl's side of the bargain in remote seclusion.

As they continued to walk among the lodges, bound for Nate's, the old mountaineer launched into an essay of how he'd come across Possum at one of the forts once and hadn't found him that bad a sort. Said he'd never seen John, but had always allowed as to how if he ran with Old Penn, "his hide wa'n't worth too many possibles . . ." But, he said, if Possum and John had turned their backs on doing Penn's evil will and joined up with Jacob Lyman, then dog bite him for a bone, if he didn't also allow as to how them two must be a shinin' pair of old coons.

Early arrivals among the lodges seemed to have strived for some kind of orderliness that later went all askew and helter-skelter. Nate and his woman, Dawn Calf, were obviously among the early-comers. Nate's lodge, a parchment-like spire of time-baked skins, sat with those in something approximating an orderly row on either side of a thirty-yard-wide strip.

Lyman had seen Nate Chapman's lodge dozens of times before, it seemed; seeing it again here was like a homecoming.

Lodges of those who came later went up wherever the travois stopped when the man of the family—if such was the case—saw an old friend and commenced his rendezvousin', while his squaw saw to pitching the lodge.

There was ample space between lodges. To keep things free inside the giant circle of his lodge floor, Nate had left most of his possibles stacked outside; most of the others did the same.

In Indian-like tradition, in front of each lodge was positioned a stick tripod from which dangled various ornaments, implements, trophies, and amulets, in this case, of Nate's medicine.

Nate led the way into his rendezvous quarters, crouching to pass awkwardly with his stick leg through the tiny opening and waving a welcome to Lyman behind him. Inside was only slightly dimmer than outside. A soft yellow glow managed to work its way through the opaque lodgeskins, and the smoke flaps at the top were spread, allowing in plenty of daylight.

Looking around him, Lyman observed that Dawn Calf had performed proper work in hacking the cured buffalo hides to a sturdy but paper-like thinness. Working with an adze-like elkhorn "dubber," she had carefully chipped off flakes of cured hide down to this wafer-thickness. He also knew these chips were saved; when boiled with water and other seasonings they'd take on the consistency of boiled potatoes and about the same bland flavor. Typical of a Crow woman's intensive industry and domestic skills, the lodge interior was tidy and clean; the exterior of the parchment-like lodgeskins were bright with reds, blues, yellows, blacks, and greens of natural dyes in provocative traditional Crow Indian design.

"Well," Nate said, "here she is." Lyman didn't know if he meant his wife or his quarters. "The robe is spread and the pipe is lit."

Dawn Calf crouched by the fire in the center of the lodge tending to the cooking meat; aromas filled the ample lodge and set Lyman's stomach to complaining about its emptiness.

Dawn Calf was a sight younger than Nate, but still the old man hadn't robbed the papoose rack, a fact evident in the crosshatch of her wrinkling smile at the return of her man and the arrival of a guest. Words, Lyman could clearly see, would have been unnecessary between the man and his wife. The peglegged mountaineer signed at the woman for their jug. She rose obediently to fetch it for him while Nate took his place as head of the lodge opposite the door. Without a word, he also signed to Lyman to take the guest's place of honor at his left in the lodge.

Lyman also knew that to pass between his host and the fire ring was an unforgivable breach of etiquette.

Only after Dawn Calf scooted to him with his vessel of gullet wash did Nate speak.

"Ya'll have a drink with me, Mr. Lyman, afore you set about your affairs of business. It's the ann-yall whing-ding, the time's shinin' to paw and root and beller." It was more a statement than an invitation. Nate poked in the jumbled pile of possessions handy beside his stack of buffalo robes that constituted his bed.

He half-filled the huge tin cup he unearthed and passed it to Lyman. Nate dug some more, found another, and doused its insides from the jug which made gulping sounds as he filled his cup.

He held up his cup in a salute to his guest. "To you, Jacob Lyman. And to those no longer with us. They was, to a man, good old toads."

Lyman half-grinned at Chapman's serious toast. "To the good old toads," he said, taking a big swig. It had been a long time since he'd tasted Alexander MacLaren's brand of grain alcohol. The effect on his palate and his vocal chords reminded him why the Indians called it firewater.

He knew, too, that Indians, before accepting whiskey in trade for furs, insisted the trader toss a thimbleful into the hearth to prove its flammable qualities by its alcohol content. If it flared up, it was accepted as proper "firewater."

"May I present Dawn Calf, my woman," Nate pronounced with exaggerated protocol.

Hearing her name and guessing at the reference, Dawn Calf fixed her eyes on Lyman from the fire and again squinted a wrinkled and shy smile at him. Typical of the Crows, Dawn Calf had once been a handsome woman. But the years of hard, slaving work in broiling sun, over smoky fires, and in bitter cold had worked their evils in her face and form.

"Proud to make you acquaintance, ma'am," Lyman said, remembering his manners. Even if she couldn't understand a word he said, she'd get the drift from his tone, he was sure.

"We have things to speak of, Mr. Lyman," Nate said. "I poured your first bolt of old brave-maker. You now know where the jug is." He thumped the brown crockery jug against the lodge floor beside him. "And be welcome."

"Obliged," Lyman said.

Chapman squared and stiffened himself in his seat on the robes, somehow giving Lyman a premonition of bad news.

"They's strange doin's afoot, Jake. I told you I'd tell you of your old pard, Lamartine. Went under. This spring. Before the beaver plews lost prime."

A quick tic of sudden grief and shock flickered across Lyman's cheek. He shuddered under it. "You got this for sure, Nate?"

"I was there. Seen him dead with these eyes."

Death was constant companion in this country. It was expected. Still when news of it came, it was never easy.

"Rene Lamartine was a good old toad," Lyman said in the simple eulogy of the mountain man. "We were free trappers, but threw together four or five seasons back. He was one to walk the trail with. Some, he was."

"Queer doin's afoot, Jake. Somethin' strange moving about in the land, queer and out of place. You'll find it out soon enough from some of Maclaren's trappers. Rene had signed on with a brigade of MacLaren's Western Fur Company last season. I come upon 'em and was persuaded to camp with 'em a few days and dip my cup in their stew pot. Rene was runnin' a beaver line some miles out. When he was two days late reportin' back to camp with his plews, I offered to make a trip up that way and keep my eyes shinin' for him. So, 'twas me come across him dead, and the place it happened undisturbed, so I had me a good chance to read clear sign. Queer doin's, Jake."

"What are you trying to tell me, Nate?"

"They's strange doin's afoot," Nate repeated, as though he would take his own good time getting down to cases. "MacLaren's company is in trouble as I read the medicine. Men missin' and no accountin' for 'em. Caches lifted and they tell me the Blackfoot sign around 'em is unmistakable. But what I saw makes me wonder. Uncommonly strange doin's."

Lyman waited. Eventually Nate would get to the point.

"And that was the way I found your pard Rene Lamartine. One Blackfoot arrer squar' in the back but his scalp not lifted. There's the catch. Got me puzzled. And whoever done it didn't know more'n a jackass about coverin' his sign. Makin' it look like the work of Blackfoot, but leavin' the scalp, and then sign in the mud and the dirt and leaves such as ary porkeater could read like a book."

"What for sign?," Lyman asked.

"Mostly favored Blackfeet mockersins, Jake. Other kinds, too. Sioux, mebbe. Uncommon, puzzlin' pair-ups of tribes. Like somebody done it of a purpose to lay blame on the Indians, any Indians. And dog bite me for a bone, Indian'll walk toe-in, we both know that. White man, particularly if he's a pilgrim and not a hivernant like you and me, walks splay-footed, like a duck.

"I've said little about it. Them of the trappers' brigade, the hull shebang of 'em, tore off up there after I carted Rene back to their camp, and in no time the con-demned idjits had tromped out all the sign. I taken to calc'latin' that if they was that dumb, they sure ain't going to listen to me tellin' 'em it wa'n't Blackfeet that put Rene Lamarine under. They'd say for certain I hadn't read the sign clear, and just chalk me up for a meddlesome old man. But you watch, Jake Lyman. You're the only one I think'd listen. You watch. Thar's queer doin's afoot."

Chapter Nine

From outside, over the murmur of rendezvous hubbub, Lyman heard a voice raised near Chapman's entry flap.

"Hello, the lodge!" The voice was John's.

Lyman glanced at Nate. It was his role to respond, not Lyman's.

"Enter if ye're of peaceful intent," Nate hailed back.

John's black grinning face appeared in the opening, sizing up the lodge's interior before entering. Behind him, Lyman could see the waist and legs of Possum.

"It's my partner, John," he told Nate. "Possum's with him."

"Well, come in, come in, the pair of ye," Nate said. "Friends of Griz-Killer Lyman is friends of Stick-Leg."

"We were told you were heading this way with Stick-Leg," John said to Lyman. "Didn't take much asking to find his lodge." The black man slid in and took a place of lesser significance between Jake Lyman's left and the lodge door. Possum followed him, squatting between John and the small, circular opening. Once inside, waiting on tradition, they didn't speak until the master of the lodge spoke to them.

"Well, Mr. Possum and Mr. Nigger John, we're obliged to share the cups, but ye'll have a drink with me and Mr. Lyman in honor of you two comin' to your senses and forsaking that scoundrel Penn. Here, Jacob, fetch me that cup. The three of ye may share it."

After Nate filled the tin vessel to the rim, Lyman passed it to John for a swig. After him, in turn, Possum also drank gratefully.

"I'm obliged for your hospitality, Mr. Chapman," John said, handing the whiskey cup back to Lyman. "But my oh my, that neck oil'd raise a blood blister on a moccasin!"

"It may of been Mr. Chapman when you was on Penn's dole, but since ye're a pard of Lyman here, it's Nate. As I was tellin' Jake, ye're welcome to the warmth of my lodge for the rendezvous and for the keepin' of your possibles. But I expect ye'll be bringin' somethin' to sweeten my cup, or some meat for the fire. Do we understand one another, Nigger John?"

Now it was Lyman's turn to speak up. "He may have been Nigger John when Penn was calling the tune, but since he's a pard of mine, it's plain John."

Chapman smiled at the obvious correction. "And that's plain, Jake. Does Possum savvy English?"

"He hasn't missed a thing you've said, Nate. He might not shine with cultured flatlander lingo, but he does well enough out here. His spoken English may not be the best, but he can put his point across with our people."

"You palaver Absaroky, Possum?" Nate asked.

Possum was taking a second pull from the cup. He brought it down prematurely and swiped a sleeve across his mouth. "Absaroka, huh! Your woman Crow? I talk her for you?"

"Wall, I was calc'latin' a bit more than that. I could keep ye in corn squeezin's for the frolic if ye could l'arn me to palaver with her in Absaroky, and start her on the white man's tongue."

Possum rubbed his big hands in anticipation. This was by far the best and most rewarding job he'd ever been offered, and the glint of delight was in his dark eyes. "What call her?"

Nate look at Lyman, puzzled.

Lyman understood and answered. "Dawn Calf."

Possum looked the woman over. "Dawn Calf. Okay name. Fine woman. Nathan Chapman got fine woman. First teach words when Nathan want fun in robes."

Nate rustled and stiffened in his seat. "Ah, no, ya don't, ye con-demned idjit! She don't need them words. I got a sign for that."

"No teach love-stuff?"

John laughed. "Nobody needs teach for that, Possum. That comes, you might say, natural."

"No, con-demn your red hide," Nate said. "I want her to know about strikin' the lodge, and puttin' it up, and mendin' my britches. Thing such as that."

Possum feigned disappointment. "Teach good words. No night talk." He spewed palaver at her in Crow, and Dawn Calf responded in understanding. He apparently told her of the plan to teach her some English. She smiled, glancing appreciatively at Nate.

John spoke. "Jake, we seen Mr. MacLaren. He knows Possum and me are riding with you now. I'm glad of that. Mr. MacLaren and Penn don't get on that well. We might of got run off from rendezvous if we wasn't with you."

Lyman sensed there was more than that in John's mention of MacLaren.

"And so, John?"

"We didn't talk long. He wants to see you after we've traded. His lodge is up by the store. I can point you to it. He wants to see you alone—he said it had something to do with your friend, Lamartine."

Lyman's eyes met Nate's briefly, a whole conversation of unspoken words passing in the glance.

"I'll attend to it directly, John. Nate, I'll round up some meat and a jug and I'll be back. We can trade any time. I better get up there and see what's on MacLaren's mind. It isn't every day an old coon like me gets an invitation to talk with the great Alexander MacLaren."

Lyman spun himself out of his cross-legged position, feeling his head spin only slightly from the power of Nate's Taos Lightnin'. He quickly regained his equilibrium. He felt a false strength filling him from the "Touse," giving him the guts to go talk with MacLaren.

He wasn't long in finding the head man of the Western Fur Company. A man of his bearing was conspicuous around the trading tables, which still bustled with activity.

Alexander MacLaren was a big man, as big as Nate Chapman must have been in his best days. MacLaren saw Lyman moving through the throngs of trading mountain men and Indians and smiled in recognition. He began to make his way to meet the mountain man. MacLaren wore a colorful wool shirt under a heavily fringed buckskin coat with long whang-fringes along the sleeve seams and in Vs down the chest and back. Each whang was decorated at various lengths by large, glassy and colorful trade beads threaded on them. Dark brown wool trousers were stuffed into good-quality boots that came halfway up his calf.

MacLaren had a strong and square Celtic face with a mane of thick red hair that sprouted far down his forehead. He was bareheaded and clean-shaven. As he reached out for Lyman's hand in greeting, he looked around to see who might overhear his words.

"Mr. Lyman," he said, his voice deep and rich with burr and with the faint, clipped quality of the Scotsman, but soft with confidential tone. "I would have a word with you. In private, if you please."

Lyman studied the big leader of the Western Fur Company. MacLaren was not only a power in St. Louis; he ruled strongly but fairly in these mountains. "One of my friends told me," he said.

"Aye. Are you finished with your commerce?"

"No, sir. All in good time. I believe I'd prefer to hear what you have to say first."

"Good. Come." MacLaren led Lyman to a large, clean-looking tipi a few steps from the traders' counters. MacLaren lifted the door flap and made a sign for Lyman to enter first. Inside, as it had been in Nate's lodge, the light coming down through the smoke flap gave a diffused, comforting glow inside the spacious quarters which MacLaren occupied alone. Lyman had no doubt that MacLaren had an abundance of female companionship in the fashionable parlors and drawing rooms of St. Louis, with their gleaming inlaid floors and massive, polished mahogany furniture — if not, as well, in its famous soft and luxurious bed chambers.

Two good rifles and a scattergun hung from thongs fastened to the lodgepoles. Clean buffalo robes filled most of the area around the fire ring. It was a clean, uncluttered, efficient rendezvous headquarters for the Western Fur Company's top man.

MacLaren took a seat at the back of the lodge, as Nate had, on a pile of robes. "Take you a place, Mr. Lyman. Near me, if you please. I will prefer that we talk quietly. I rarely take whiskey before late afternoon. There's some fine and fresh coffee warm beside the fire. Please be my guest."

Lyman grabbed a convenient large tinned cup and poured it full of the hot coffee, called "black soup" by the mountain men. He waited for MacLaren to proceed.

"You're young, Mr. Lyman. You've been in these mountains a few seasons. I hear good reports of you. You harvest a fine abundance of furs each season, and cure them well. That's important, and says something about the man. We get so many plews in trade only to find out later they are worthless because of poor care. Your products are an exception, Mr. Lyman."

"Thank you, sir."

"And, I'm told, something of a legend has grown up around you. Is it true what I hear about a superb shot on a grizzly?"

"Probably exaggerated, if I know how campfire tales grow, Mr. MacLaren. I was extremely fortunate."

"You saved a white woman who'd escaped the Indians. What's become of her?"

Lyman felt sudden embarrassment. "She stays in comfortable quarters a week to ten days east. There's the matter of a young son taken from her husband, an officer in the dragoons, who was killed five years ago. I'm trying to help her find trace of him."

"He's a captive?"

"I expect so. I assume it was Cheyennes, but he could have been traded or stolen several times by now."

"It's a big country, Mr. Lyman. If still alive, he could be anywhere."

"Yes, but word travels fast, proved by the fact that you knew about the grizzly. I intend to ask around and pass the word during this encampment."

"Anything I can do to help, you have only to ask. But I asked you to come by on another matter."

"Yes, sir. Your concern about my former partner, Lamartine, wasn't it?"

"Word travels fast, as you say, Jacob. I would ask you to join my company."

"That I'd prefer not to do, Mr. MacLaren. I've been a free trapper all along, and doing well at it. No disrespect, sir, but I propose to keep it that way."

"It's not as a trapper that I need you, Jacob. And please call me Alex." Lyman was surprised at the sudden informality. "We have a problem. I need a good man out here. Of all of them, of those not already associated with me, you possess what I need in a man."

"I appreciate that, Alex. But what problem? I fail to

understand." For the moment, he held back on what he knew of the suspicions Nate had related.

"I wouldn't have you in here, Jake, if I did not feel totally comfortable in talking with you about this."

"I'd gain nothing by passing on anything talked about between us, Alex."

"Good. Something sinister is going on. I believe there's a link to the death of your friend, Lamartine. You've seen Chapman. He found Lamartine, as you may know."

Lyman nodded, still holding back what Nate had told him.

"I believe he was killed because he was a Western Fur Company man," MacLaren said.

"It was a Blackfoot arrow, but his scalp wasn't taken. This much I know," Lyman said.

"Then you are suspicious as I am, Jacob. The reports I've received these last few months I passed off as happenstance. Great risk attends this fur business, Jacob, to men as well as to belongings. But the Western Fur Company is suddenly faring much worse than other companies. The Lamartine incident isn't the first mysterious disaster. More than the usual number of our caches have been pilfered. It may come as a surprise, but Lamartine was the third of my men in as many months to die for reasons that cannot be explained. I suspect conspiracy here, Jacob. The looting of the West has always been fair game for the East. I suspect more sinister implications in all this than mere local greed and brutality."

Lyman sucked in his breath. "I didn't know. You really ought to talk with Chapman. He told me that before the men of your brigade went up to where Rene died and disturbed the ground, he found evidence of several styles of moccasins. And he believes white men wore them—at least some did."

"Aha! The plot thickens, does it? I would like to talk with your friend Chapman. Can he be trusted?"

"Nate Chapman has a big mouth, but he can also be sworn to confidence. I think of anyone I know, he can get more information without the other fellow knowing he's spilling the beans. And he was upset over Lamartine's death. We all were friends."

MacLaren cleared his throat; his emotions were close to the surface. "From experience, I know there are thieves and cutthroat killers all around us. It must be expected in this business. Also, it is not the most cordial business. Men are bound to be lost . . . to Indians . . . to exposure. A company also has to be prepared that a certain number of cached fur packs will disappear. The Western Fur Company, for months now, has been experiencing more than its share. It's gotten to the point that it's so evident, it's painful.

"Normally, if one of our trappers turns up missing in a season, it's a calculated risk. They desert, or a river gets them, or a catamount . . . lots of reasons. And what's a few buried furs? Somebody is bound to be forgetful of where they were buried, or maybe an Indian party or a clutch of thieves stumbles onto a cache. So what?

"The other two killed, aside from Lamartine, were also dead from Blackfoot arrows, but unscalped. In their cases, they were far, far from base camp, and Lord knows how many plews disappeared. Others of my company trappers returned to their caches to come to rendezvous and found open holes. It's going to show up in my tallies this year. I can sustain the loss, no problem there. But it can't go on. There's been some grumbling in the ranks. Men are talking about leaving, that there's a hex on the Western Fur Company. I need someone with a keen eye and a sharp ear. I mean to get at the root of this. Assuredly it won't do for me to do it myself. I need someone with a familiar face working in here, someone who can quietly go about his business and gather in information."

Lyman refilled his coffee cup, absorbed in what he'd heard so far from MacLaren. "If what you say is true, Alex, and if this person or persons was responsible for killing

Rene, you've found your man. I don't have any particular loyalty to you, but there is the point that I have respect for you as a fair and decent man. For those reasons, I'll do it. But there is one problem."

"Which is?"

"My partners. An Indian named Possum and a black man called John. They rode with Thomas Penn until last year. There was a confrontation over my stolen traps. Penn and I both were wounded, but I succeeded in running him off, tail between his legs. Out of it, Possum and John allied themselves with me. Penn's a scoundrel, but I can't imagine he's mixed up in your problem. Penn's certainly capable of it, but he doesn't think that big. Not on his own. He lives off petty crime. John and Possum would know. They've never said anything, and we've talked a lot about their experiences with Penn. The plain truth is I've never liked him, and after what happened between us, and what Possum and John have told me, I regard him even less."

"Hmmm. And now they ride with you?"

"Yes, sir. As full partners. I'll not sever my relationship with them. In other words, they'll have to be party to this, too."

"Do you think they'll want to be, Jake?"

Lyman took a deep breath and squared his shoulders. Possum and John would spend a lot of years living down their association with Thomas Penn. "Alex, I don't take the trail with anyone I don't trust, and I mean fully trust. As you say, this is a mean business in a mean country. A man picks well the men he works with and associates with. Need I say more?"

"You needn't. But broach it with them carefully, Jacob. There are risks to be taken. We can't expect gentlemanly conduct of our adversaries."

"We three can take care of ourselves, Alex. Possum and John are decent men."

"You'll get farthest by signing on as my trappers, and letting it be known that you are. I dislike making a target of you, Jacob. But you see the wisdom of the maneuver."

"I do. I've a score to settle with someone for Rene Lamartine's death. I'll talk with Possum and John. I think I should also tie up with Nate Chapman."

"If he'll do it, I think that's wise."

"You should talk with him, though. Hear what he has to say about what he found where Lamartine was murdered. He's got a keen eye for sign and it told him quite a story."

"Sounds like a good man. I'll do it. We'll talk again before rendezvous is over, Jacob. I believe you'll quickly get to the root of the problem."

Lyman got up and started to leave.

"Godspeed, Jacob Lyman," MacLaren said.

Chapter Ten

The conversations with Nate and MacLaren, and the shock of the news of Rene's death dogged Lyman the rest of the afternoon.

With nightfall, the breeze that had trifled with the land during the day died with the darkness. The roar of rendezvous settled into a lulling murmur, and the shooting was done with again until daylight. Above Lyman, a moon-bleached night was shot full of stars. On the land around him, everywhere he looked, rendezvous fires flickered against the dark like rubies tossed on ebony velvet.

Around the fires, he could see men hovering, drinking and talking.

At his own fire, old Nate Chapman nursed his can of snakehead whiskey, drinking steady but slow. He didn't mow it away like the others did, out of respect for the backbreaking cost and the horrendous aftermath.

Just now Nate hitched the splintered and weatherbeaten old pegleg under his good one to sit crosslegged with the others around the flames. The glow of it danced on the face of Possum, his handsome, impassive redman features holding anticipation. John, his black skin lost in the dark aside from shiny highlights, showed white, well-placed teeth, and his great gleaming orbs of eyes with their dark-brown pupils.

Possum and John sat together at the gossip-fire. There was a smattering of others, maybe a half-dozen. Lyman knew most of them by name, but didn't have much other memory to connect them to.

"Jake," Nate said, pointing his tale-spinning at Lyman, but intending it for those clustered at the fire ring. "You recollect old Jack de Fonville that I run with back some seasons? Old de Fonville went under after the frolic of '34, wa'n't it? Old Jack de Fonville was some, he was. There was a man to ride the river with, if ever there was one."

More than small talk, Nate was building to a whopper. Lyman looked at Chapman, his eyes agreeing. It was more than reflected fire that sparkled in the old one-legged coon's eyes, bright as they were, and alert with merriment. Lyman glanced at the other mountaineers around the fire. Most of them probably hadn't known Nate enough to be aware that he was about to uncork enough manure to enrich several acres.

"It been a coon's age ago that old de Fonville taken a Arikara arrer in the hip that stove him up considerable. De Fonville and me was with Major Ashley and them goin' up the Misery River in the keelboats in '23. Waugh! Them Arikaras let us know it was time to paint for war. And we did. Such a fight I never been in. Them Arikaras you could never tame to the plow in a hell of a sight. They never know'd how to raise nothin' but hell and hair.

"Old Jack de Fonville was all mountaineer. Full of brag and fight as a old razorback stroppin' hisself agin a rock. Never was a hand to whimper, though, by God, he had just cause. With that hip lamin' him up to a fare-thee-well, he had to go back on downriver to get knit up and for a time had hisself hitched to a calico woman and took up farmin' near Sa'nt Louie.

"Old de Fonville was the most onpredictable cuss. He'd give you the shirt off his back while figuring a way to steal your possibles. Onpredictable! I mind the time him and me was crossin' the Platte in a bullboat. Skinned us out a buffler and with bent willer sticks had made up one of them floatin' bowls with the hide stitched and caulked around. About as pesky to handle as tryin' to put a bridle on the wind.

"That damned bullboat was spinnin' and pitchin' around. About halfway acrost, that cumberous old boat done one of its con-demned dips and some of our possibles liked to spilt out. I made a grab for the stuff, and my horn and pouch slid off my shoulder. Spang! Straight to the bottom they went.

"Old Jack know'd I'd be right up against it without my powder and galena balls and such, so he jumps up and yells he'll get 'em for me. Jack puts down his oar and leaps in and sunk to the bed of the Platte like as rock. About that time, the boat skates over close to the shore, so I beached 'er and stood there waitin' for old de Fonville to surface.

"After a long enough while I took to calc'latin' that I'd best get about savin' my pardner. In them sit'ations, a man's got to do what he can. I jumped in and swam around a bit and finally found him down there.

"Don't you know that there the thievin' son of a she-wolf sat, on the bottom of the Platte, tryin' to pour the powder outten my horn into his'n!"

A ripple of amusement circled the fire.

"We was a pair, and that's for sure. Me gimpin' around with this here stick-leg and Jack with that lamed-up hip of his makin' him walk like any minute he's fixin' to fall down.

"That time he was down below there a couple seasons or three, him and that calico woman kept a coop full of chickens, besides raisin' what groceries they needed. One time there come up one of those wild tarnatious dust-funnel tornado winds they get back there. A blue norther is like a whisper up alongside one of them. Black she was and howlin' like a banshee, big at the top way up in the sky, and screwin' down small at the bottom and pickin' up ever'thin' in sight. Plowed a trough a mile wide across ever'thin' it touched, right down to bare dirt and rocks. That was some wind, that was.

"Jack said it picked up trees and cabins and cattle and people and some of 'em it kilt and some of 'em it set right down nice as you please as much as a quarter of a mile away without leavin' a mark on 'em. Jack said at one place, it flung a man's haystack straight into a tree leavin' all the straws stickin' straight outta the wood like bristles on a hog's back. Jack said he had notions about cuttin' that tree down and makin' it up into hair brushes.

"But he had other things on his mind. Like that flock of chickens he and his woman had worked so hard to raise. When the dust settled, they found that most of the chickens was dead, and being the frugal little person she was, Jack's woman cleaned most of them and preserved and dried the meat and made up pemmican and whatever she could.

"But there was some of them that had come th'ough without a scratch, others of 'em had broken wings and broken legs and such.

"Jack knew more than a little by now about hurt legs, him with one of his own. He took the hurt ones into the cabin and patched 'em up as best he could and whittled him some splints and bound up them broken wings and broken legs on those miserable little cusses.

"Jack had a gentle side to him when it come to hurt animals.

"By and by, as the birds got to feelin' better, they put 'em back out in the chicken yard.

"But it was the funniest thing. The wind had blown most of their feathers off, and Jack's woman commence to notice they was gettin' sunburnt. By this time, she and Jack'd put a lot of work into keepin' them alive and healthy, so she got down a bolt of her calico cloth and made 'em up little shirts and britches like old Jack wore to pertect 'em.

"She fixed up a special nice suit of clothes for their rooster, thinkin' it'd make him feel better because he had a broken leg and had to be gimpin' around the hens kind of crippled up that way.

"By and by, one of their neighbors come up with his team and wagon and saw that rooster struttin' around the chicken yard still like the cock of the walk with that splint on his leg and sportin' that bright-printed suit of clothes.

"He commenced to laugh like hell. 'What're you laughin' at?' Jack asks his neighbor.

"'Why, that's the funniest thing I ever saw, that rooster hobbling around with that splint on his leg and wearin' that calico suit.'

"'Hey,' Jack says. 'That ain't funny. What's funny is when that son of a bitch he tries to hold a hen down with that splint on his leg and get them calico britches off with the other!'"

Chapter Eleven

After a night of scouting the perimeter of the trappers' camp
and positioning the renegade forces for their ambush, Skull,
and the ragtag kid that always traipsed along after him like a
hound broken by the whip, came back in to report to Thomas
Penn. As they moved through the mesh of trees ringing the
protected circle of clearing where Penn had set up his command post, the early morning light danced off Skull's hairless
dome.

Winter's bite was already gnawing the land this morning.
Small scoops of snow shifted in the cups of brittle leaves like
fine sand as the wind toyed with it.

The pallid Skull never wore a hat or cap because they
constantly slithered around his bald knob of head, or
whipped away in the wind with no thatch of hair to secure
them.

Something had robbed Skull of his ability to grow hair.
There were those who said it happened after he caught the
pox from a St. Louis riverfront woman, or maybe a slovenly
squaw. He had no body hair either, on his chest or in a wedge
above his genitals; he never had to shave. The bony bridges
above his deepset and sinister dark eyes were also hairless.

Lean as long-dried and long-stored jerky, Skull walked in
his effortless way to where Thomas Penn—a huge man

crouched with his greatcoat slung over his shoulders like a cape—warmed himself at a fire and watched with interest. Studying him with eyes expert in judging evil, Penn marked again a face that was dry-looking and spare of flesh. From weather and wind, it had shrunk—so tight that it shone—around temples, cheekbones, jaws, and chin. Skull's lips were thin, his mouth wide.

Skull spoke with a perpetual, humorless grin—more the leer of a confident killer who could have your scalp before you knew he was in your camp. His white, well-set teeth added to his skull-like appearance. His true name had long since been lost, or conveniently forgotten to avoid a dark and questionable past. Some said he was Mexican or Portuguese; Skull never owned up to any of it.

Though Skull's cadaverous frame held not an ounce of spare flesh, he possessed relentless and almost feverish energies whether scouting, hunting, or killing. Penn credited himself with enormous good judgment in enlisting Skull after the encounter with Jacob Lyman deprived him of his two pawns, John and the Indian, Possum.

In joining Penn, Skull dragged along the miserable young white wretch known as Orphan. Where Skull had found him, no one knew or dared ask; not even Penn, who cared little. Penn considered children worthless and ineffectual. He largely ignored the sulking Orphan, hardly acknowledging the lackluster but quick-tempered adolescent Skull kept to cook and perform other squaw work and dirty, menial jobs.

Orphan was unpredictable, erupting without warning from sullen brooding silence to a tempest of insane rage. Still, Skull maintained a powerful hold on the child, who bowed without question to Skull's every whim. As Skull's ready apprentice in things bloody and brutal, Orphan had adopted the eyes and hair-trigger violence of a natural killer. He remembered little of his native tongue, responding only in a polyglot of English and gutteral grunts of Cheyenne dialects.

Penn warmed himself in Skull's fierce loyalty, finding him a worthy ally after the cowardly defection of John and Possum to that scum, Lyman. Penn pondered it; he cared little for those two as it was. Lyman was stuck with them now. He himself, Penn thought, needed men with courage and deadly daring, willing to slit a throat or take a scalp if it brought in money. Big money. Some day, he vowed, he'd return home to England in triumph and glory and shake his mighty fist at those who had banished him from his ancestral home.

His chance to realize his destiny came when he was approached to embark on a secret mission to destroy Alexander MacLaren's powerful Western Fur Company. In doing so, he was promised a significant share in the company that would move into the void. Almost as if by divine intercession, Penn found Skull. Skull responded by recruiting a band of paid low-life white freebooters to destroy MacLaren's major force in the beaver country—the brigade of trappers led by two Western Fur Company *bourgeois* Kern Abbott and Zebulon Broadus.

Before dawn, Penn and Skull had crouched close to a warming fire as Penn ordered the scouting mission. "We must be certain it's Abbott and Broadus down there," Penn insisted. "No guessing. No hunches."

Skull spread a thin-lipped grin. "Me'n Orphan'll find out."

"My New York associates will tolerate no blunders. We're paid, Skull—and handsomely—to destroy MacLaren's fur enterprise. We must not jeopardize their support by needlessly sacrificing men of other fur companies. You and that shiftless waif owe your livelihood to that."

Now Skull returned from the scout at his fast clip to where Penn crouched by the fire. The renegade veered to a pile of possibles by the hasty lean-to where Penn had spent a bitter-cold night and began searching. He grunted when he found a shiny-gray jug.

Skull could—and desired to—drink any time, any place, morning or night, in the blazing sun or burrowed in a snowdrift. His capacity for the commodity called coffin varnish was prodigious.

Wordlessly, Skull bent down opposite Penn, working the cork free of the jug. He whirled the vessel on his crooked arm and poured a long swig down his throat without so much as letting the taste linger. Skull seemed to need it for warmth this morning as the frigid bite of breeze nipped at his bare head with frosty teeth.

Skull swung the jug up in an offer to Orphan, who grabbed for it. Gripping its slick sides, Orphan drained some of the contents, making gurgling sounds with his mouth. He handed the jug back to Skull with an expression of gratitude. Skull had taught the boy his own special tricks, Penn observed. Orphan was almost as much of a genius with the jug as Skull was. Skull had another swig. He set the unstoppered jug down, suggesting there was no call to cork it when he'd need another drink in a minute or so.

"Well . . .?" Thomas Penn said, impatient for Skull's report.

"I suspect it's Abbott and Broadus with thirty or more of MacLaren's trappers, Thomas," he said, in an unexpectedly deep bass voice and with a characteristic directness. As mentally bright as he was vicious, Skull was a man who used his mind much and his mouth little.

"Must you have that offensive creature beside you all the time?" Penn asked. "Doesn't he have things to do elsewhere? We have matters to discuss and this isn't child's play. He may drink like a man, but he's far from being one."

In obedience to his superior, Skull's eyes flashed on the dejected- and rejected-looking Orphan who stood, shoulders stooped and vacant-eyed, a few steps away. "Here! You!" Skull commanded sharply. "Take my rifle back to where our possibles is. Make sure it's loaded and ready to fire, and see to the prime of your own fuzee. And do anything else you got to do. But lay low. You're going to get your chance to get some hair for your scalp stick this day, Orphan."

The young man shook his head as if he had been daydreaming before Skull spoke to him. Orphan possessed long, unkempt and stringy hair, almost as if to make up for what Skull lacked. Orphan was only fastidious, after the Indian fashion, about his facial hair. He had a nervous, irritating fetish for stroking his cheeks and jaw with his dirty, long-nailed fingers. Despite his fair complexion, his face had not yet had much of the soft down of young manhood. Still, if Orphan felt a wisp of fuzz sprouting, out came his primitive clamshell tweezers and without benefit of a looking glass, he plucked out the offending bristle without a wince. Orphan looked at Skull blankly and then cat-eyed at Thomas Penn, backed off a few steps, turned and disappeared into the cold forest.

"The boy'll make a good accounting of himself, Thomas," Skull said. "I taught him good."

Orphan's presence had been a constant irritation to Thomas Penn. "He's your responsibility, Skull. Personally, I don't trust infants. If he makes some kind of dimwit mistake, of which he's perfectly capable, the fat's in the fire. This is ticklish business."

"Orphan does like I tell him. I told you, I taught him well."

"The camp down there, what about it? You're sure it's Abbott and Broadus out of MacLaren's company. We're not being paid to trifle with other companies. Suspicions don't count, Skull. Before we commit the men to an attack we must be sure."

Skull's voice carried an edge of impatience. "All right, take my word for it. Me and the boy didn't see Abbott and Broadus, that's all. I saw others that I know are with them this season. They're all sittin' ducks. A dozen or more went out before light to check traps. I've men stalking each of them.

When they hear the attack start, those dozen or so are as good as dead meat."

"And it will look like the work of the Blackfeet?"

"Dammit!" Skull spit out the word, growing angrier over Penn's apprehensions. "The way we planned it. This job will be carried out with enough bows and arrows to look like a Blackfoot war party. There are just enough muskets and rifles to make sure there are no slip-ups."

"No survivors," Thomas Penn said in a sardonic tone.

"No survivors. Well, maybe we can leave one with just enough life to get to a post and blame it on the Blackfeet. No way we'll be found out."

"None of them saw you and Orphan while you were scouting?"

Skull looked at his boss through tight eyes. "Damn! What does it take to convince you, Penn? What you got me working for you for if not to get the job done right? We could of brought hair if I hadn't worried about tipping our hand. We was that close. No, they didn't see us."

"The men are in position for the attack?"

Skull was resigned to the endless questions. "You have only to give the signal."

With the first sunlight flooding the sky, Skull and Orphan had watched from hiding as the camp began to stir. Already a dozen of its trappers were off checking the night's catch. The pair's reconnaissance of the trappers' camp, however, had missed one major factor, a quartet of newcomers. . . . Lately joining the Western Fur Company and attached to the brigade of Abbott and Broadus a few weeks after the last rendezvous, were Jacob Lyman and Penn's former confederates Possum and John, and the seasoned and woods-wise Nate Chapman.

In the camp that was the target of the impending attack, Possum ladeled hot and thick breakfast broth from the brigade pot into his huge whiskey cup and came over to where Jacob Lyman squatted by his warming fire.

The season was again laying hard on the land. The air around the camp was cold and still. The sun made its usual bulge of fire over the range to the east, any warmth from its light absent as the creatures of the land arose. It was coming on to robe season again, a time to cache warm, to winter over again until the thaw. Lyman thought about Rachel and was pestered by thoughts of being close again to her warm body. He shook his head angrily at the lust already building in him. It wasn't good for a man to think this way. The previous summer, he had helped John and Possum build their ample but snug cabin nearby, but a respectable distance from his and Rachel's home. Maybe, he thought, some day they'd have their own women too . . . Nate Chapman did.

Nate would return alone to Crow country and winter over with Dawn Calf's village.

Nagging thoughts also disturbed Lyman—he would return to Rachel with discouraging word about young Daniel. He had learned of several boys matching Daniel's description in Cheyenne camps. Investigation only showed that one had died, one had been liberated and returned to his family, a third traded and since stolen from his foster tribe and apparently vanished, as far as anyone knew.

The news he had to take to Rachel was hardly warming. The weather wasn't helping. Already, an early freeze was in the air. It clutched the land with a bitter grip that wasn't going to give up without a fight.

With the death of the leaves, and all trees but the pines standing veined and naked against a depressing sky, the land had become even more raw and more lonesome. Spring and the spreading lushness of the land of summer made Lyman feel big in the chest, his legs somehow longer. Winter, by contrast, got down inside and shrunk and shriveled him. This winter's coming was already working its evil and he wouldn't feel himself again until he was back in his warm cabin and in Rachel's arms.

There were those damned visions of Rachel again, he thought.

The Lyman party, with its new member Nate Chapman, joined the Abbott and Broadus brigade after rendezvous, all of them now fanning out from the base camp to trap nearby. With winter coming on, all but baring its fangs, the trappers who had worked the far-flung rivers converged back at base.

They were pulling in the last of the precious furs before plunging hell-bent through new snow for the sanctuary and warmth of a Western Fur Company fort while the weather called a halt to everything. There they, too, would winter over.

After rendezvous, Lyman, John, Possum, and Nate had trapped without brigade affiliation, though getting the word out that they had allied themselves with MacLaren. After several months of unsuccessfully making themselves targets of anticipated renegade attacks, they set out to find and attach themselves to one of MacLaren's brigades.

Stumbling across some of the Abbott-Broadus outriders in the lonesome and cold land, the four reported to the brigade booshways, settled into the routines of camp life and set about trapping like bona-fide MacLaren *engagees*.

The big news from Abbott and Broadus was that the annual fur jamboree next year would be at Bear Lake. Lyman knew it, had rendezvoused there before. In his mind he was already tracing his steps from the cabin and Rachel over the easiest, most direct route when the grass again sprouted green and lush and the warm sun spread its welcome blanket over the land. Then he'd again feel like the man he was, the man heading for rendezvous.

Watching Possum stride over to join him, Lyman was again struck by the handsome features of the so-called aborigine. There was almost a delicacy in the fine structure of the Indian's face—the smooth, unlined, unpocked skin that carried the hue of good bronze. Given a proper suit of clothes and a cultured haircut—and a bit more instruction with the white man's lingo—Possum could easily become the toast of two continents.

But, Lyman mused, as Possum crouched beside him and warmed his hands with his cup of hot, meaty brew, that would be unfair. Possum belonged here in the wild, open country. He didn't need to be chained up like a dog, or walled in like some wild beast in a zoo.

"Crow bird him caw in night," Possum said, as if searching for something to pass the time of day. He pursed his well-formed lips around the hot rim of the cup. He slurped in a measure and swallowed. "Bad medicine."

The wind, picking up around them, sent the steam from his cup slanting away, suggesting the winter storms that were so close a man could almost see them. The winds of winter would soon pick up in earnest, shrill and perverse, Lyman thought, rattling the gaunt branches of trees and keening their dirge as they combed the rocks in the high places. Lyman didn't like winter.

Lyman grinned. "Sure as hell." It was an old Indian superstition; death was near if a crow cawed after dark. "Smart crows are down around Taos this time of year where it'll be a sight warmer. Dumb ones up here sit in the trees at night yelling their heads off about cold feet."

"Jacob's joke dumb. Maybe these crows wear moccasins."

"Absaroky? Crow Indians?"

"Huh! Even when Jacob talk straight he talk *mah-son-ne*, dumb. No Absaroka here." He waved with his cup. "Long, long, far, far Absaroka. Crow people. Nathan's people. Dawn Calf. Possum think man out there want to sound like bird. Sign to others of camp to attack. Like we wait for since you talk at big trade with White Chief MacLaren."

"An attack? Come on, Possum. In this weather?" Lyman jerked his head up and studied the land, the tallest mountains rising blue and cold in the west against a winter-solemn sky. Already new snow lay patched on their slopes.

The foothills were all around and suddenly Lyman felt hemmed in and trapped, as if there was no escape. Premonitions of evil chilled his bones. He felt as though he was in the bottom of a kettle; he'd heard how easy it was to shoot fish in a barrel.

"Crow still don't caw at night. Bad medicine. Man sign, it."

"Maybe it was some of the trappers."

Possum's eyes flashed on Lyman. He didn't have the words to express his true fears, and that made him angry at Lyman's apparent stupidity. "Not these men. Not friends. Man out there. Many." He waved his cup again, making a crude circle in the air. "Man all around. In hills. Behind trees. Come when most friends go to traps. Like now. You see. Come for scalp, maybeso. Then take furs, guns. Possum smell white-eyes. Long time with Penn. Know Penn smell, him. Penn there. Hide in trees." Possum again waved his cup describing the hills that fringed and closed in the trappers' camp.

The goddam surround at last, Lyman thought, panic and anger prodding him. And Penn at the root of it? "Dammit, Possum, if you thought that why didn't you say so sooner? I've got to alert Abbott and Broadus. You start rousin' the others-tell 'em to fort up and get ready."

As he leaped away to race to find the brigade leaders, Lyman heard a muffled gunshot a good distance off and losing its volume as it fought its way around through trees and brush to bring its alarm to the ear. Sound traveled that way this time of year. The mountains themselves, so full of life otherwise, seemed still and dead. Death was somehow present.

Chapter Twelve

A good fifty yards away, in a dense stand of trees, Lyman found Kern Abbott emerging out of the booshways' lodge, puzzlement smeared over his face. He, too, had heard the shot.

"I think we're under attack, Kern," Lyman yelled, almost breathlessly. The head of Zeb Broadus poked out the lodge door, with the same quizzical expression. As though the first shot had been a signal, the sounds of gunfire from other sectors around the camp floated to the ears of the three at the lodge.

"Possum heard somebody passing sign to one another that way all night."

Abbott's head jerked in a sudden fury. "Well, why in hell didn't he say something right off?" Abbott was a big man, long-armed and long-legged with a body that seemed built for the gun and not the other way around. His face reflected a seasoning and an experience in the ways of the wild mountains. Like other mountaineers who'd survived to become hivernants, Kern Abbott possessed busy eyes and an alert, untroubled face.

Broadus now stepped out of the lodge, a short, egg-shaped little man who Lyman knew normally had a quick sense of humor. The lines of his face, his easy wrinkles of smile, were traced by a lifetime of good nature. Abbot was less inclined toward quick laughter.

Now Broadus' sense of the humorous had forsaken him. "I hope your Indian's not in on this with them, Lyman." Suspicion rang in his voice. "You four just showed up here of late . . . and now this. It don't look none too good."

Lyman felt the hackle hair on the back of his neck start to itch. "Zeb, if I didn't know you better, I'd take that personally. Don't ask me why Possum didn't say anything until just now. But, believe me, it has nothing to do with loyalty."

Broadus dropped it. "Thank God only half the men are out seeing to the traps. They're gritty as fish eggs rolled in sand—with them gunshots they'll be fortin' up."

Around them, the remainder of the trappers in the camp were coming alert. Without awaiting orders, they were forming a protective perimeter defense around the camp. MacLaren's trappers were picked for their abilities to think clearly in tight situations.

These were men, Lyman thought, who knew how to die standing up.

He studied Abbott's weather-darkened face, drawn with the sudden tension and threat. "I'd better go find my rifle and see to its prime," Lyman said.

Broadus nodded. "Keep your eye shinin', Jake."

"Don't blame Possum for any of this—or me. Expect that John—and Possum—will fight just as hard as any of the rest before their lamp's blown out. Let me know if there's anything more I can do. Just now I better get up there and fix to fight." He loped away. A bullet twanged through the trees close to the two leaders as they watched Lyman move away. Instinctively they scrambled for a shallow protected pocket next to their lodge.

"We picked this place good as a base for beaver, Zeb," Abbott said. "But is sure as hell don't shine for making a stand such as this." Away from the comforting warmth of their lodge, Abbott could feel the cold working its way through his blanket-like Hudson's Bay capote and the thick buckskins beneath. He glanced through the trees at the dirty white clouds above them, the sky filling up with winter storm, ready to burst like a bag too full of rocks. The sky seemed to be closing down on them, gray and leaden-looking to its very limits, unruffled and heavy in spite of the chill wind that fretted with the land.

Abbott spoke again, his lips stiff and bloodless with cold. "*They're* up and moving around in those woods and that'll keep their blood going. *They* can afford fires if need be. We sure as hell can't tend any fires. The men won't freeze, but this cold is enough to make them miserable."

"Snow's comin'," Broadus said, his round face blanched with chill. "Hard as hell to work a rifle with your fingers froze." His breath came as puffs of white frost. For now the sky held back the snow . . . it was just pure cold. Cold as hell on the stoker's day off, Zeb Broadus thought. Around them another kind of storm swirled. A hot blizzard of lead.

Within minutes, the outriding trappers straggled in amid barrages of gunshots from the slopes commanding the broad, flat, and open base camp. Every round coming in was met by a blazing scythe of answering fire from the entrenched brigade of Abbott and Broadus.

Their defense was effective but it was getting them no place. They were nailed down to their positions. Abbott and Broadus, who had ventured out in opposite directions to check their forces and assess the situation, met back at their protective depression in the land.

"What's the tally?" Broadus asked. Against a cold-ruddy face, the dark whiskers of his rounded cheeks were lightly tinted white with frost.

"Three known dead, two missing of them that went out before daylight."

"Caught us with our butts bare to the wind and that's for certain," Broadus said.

"Four wounded already. Jenkins the worst. Leaned against a galena pill goin' past and got gut-shot. He won't make it. Some of them Indians has some old fuzees, too, trade muskets probably. Evans took a big ball in the hip. Looks broke. He might as well of got hit with a swivel gun."

"Hell!" Broadus said, his jowls a-quiver. "Those men got to be looked after. Bring 'em up here to the lodge and assign somebody to care for them. Can't do it out there with them arrows and balls comin' in. This is a bad one, Kern, and this cold ain't helpin' none."

"We got about twenty-five men left on the line, countin' Lyman and them. The weather is fixing to be meaner than a bear with two cubs and a sore tail. Damn Blackfeet on the prod, or I'm pore bull. Same ones as got Ramsey and Lamartine and that other old coon, forget his name."

"There's a limit to how long we can stand to the line like this. What'll we do?"

Abbott's eyes studied the distance as if measuring it through tight lids. "I say charge the bastards, all horns and rattles. Go after them. That's the only force they understand. Else they'll hold us here till we freeze. It ain't going to get any warmer. When it does, there ain't going to be nothing here but bones for the grass to grow up through."

"We still got cooked meat, and water in this cold ain't the worry it'd be if it was hot. We can make a stand here, Kern. But this cold is working against us. That alone'll wind up puttin' us under if the Indians don't."

"Sure won't be able to have night fires when it gets dark neither. They'll move in close and pick up off agin the light," Abbott said.

"Then let's get 'em the hell out of here! Better a man dies lookin' 'em straight in the eye than like a pup rollin' his belly up to the sky like we are now. How do you figure it, Kern?"

"Split the men into thirds. A couple of the wounded can still shoot. That'll give us enough able-bodied men in two parties to storm out of here, break their line in two places, and still leave a good force in camp."

"One of us lead 'em, or both?"

"I don't think so. I'll die before I'll ask another man, but that ain't the point. If they come up short, we ought to be here to figure what to do next. I'm thinking of Jake Lyman and one of those that's with him. Lyman's never been one to shirk a fight."

"But his one partner's that Indian of Penn's."

"By God, Zeb, don't mention that to Jake. Possum's out there fighting just now like one of us. Him and Jake and the black man are down there, shoulder to shoulder, layin' fire faster'n any five of the others. Don't sell them boys short. If old Chapman had two legs, he'd take his share of hair. He still could."

"I think it's be a mistake sendin' the Indian out against his own kind, face-to-face, Kern."

"Give one bunch to Lyman, the other to John. That's good. Bust loose out of opposite sides of the camp if they can, split the Indians. That'll put the moccasin on the other foot. Old Nate Chapman can be ornrier than a bull with sore ears, but he plays hell movin' fast on that stick leg. Leave him here; he can load and fire faster'n any two men."

The prospect excited the usually lively Broadus. "Then, by God, let's get Jake in here and get this thing going. It'll be dark in a matter of hours and come mornin' we'll all be dead from ball or the freeze."

The word was passed and Jacob Lyman crouched low and sprinted to where Abbott and Broadus waited. His hands were black from the charge after charge he had stoked down his big Hawken rifle. He had transferred some of the smudge to his face as he rubbed it to restore circulation to his cheeks.

"Jake," Abbott said, "we're about of a mind to take the warpath. We're about close enough to hell to smell smoke, and just now a little heat would be welcome. But not that much. Bein' cached down here under their guns ain't going to work. Zeb and me figure if we could drive two wedges through the Indians out there, we'd stand a chance of spooking them and sending them flying."

"Attack in two places?"

"Look, we're surrounded, no escape. Except as we hack our way out. Zeb and me are booshways, leaders in one way, but we ain't neither of us great shakes as fighters. The others of ours got their share of sand as fighters, but ain't a one a real leader. Well, what we're askin', I guess, is if you and John would lead the attack."

Zeb Broadus spoke up. "We gotta start us a backfire. Indians, even Blackfoot, respect force and fight. Go out screamin' and shakin' your fist under their nose, and they're likely to back off."

Lyman turned serious. "Don't count on it. I've a strong hunch you'll find more white faces out there than Blackfeet."

Broadus found a smile, catching Lyman's intentional pun.

"Meaning?" Abbott asked.

Lyman decided to come clean. "Renegades. Probably whites. Some Indians. I had a secret meeting with Mr. MacLaren at rendezvous. He's put two and two together; somebody's out to bring down his company. I say it's Penn. Until now I couldn't conceive that a small-time cutthroat like Thomas Penn would think big enough to mount an assault on his own against the strength of anything as big as MacLaren's Western Fur Company."

"Mr. MacLaren was uneasy at the last fur frolic about Lamartine and the others," said Abbott. "If it's Penn, somebody put him up to it. It's bigger'n him. He's takin' somebody's wages and I'll bet my plews on that."

"Penn preys on the weak and the outnumbered," Lyman

agreed. "He wouldn't risk his scalp on a venture this big on his own hook. Taking on a whole fur company's something Thomas would have no stomach for. Somebody's paying him and I'll bet that somebody's mighty big. Out east . . . New York . . . maybe European. But, no time now to get into that. I figure we've got to take the bull by the horns and bust out of here!"

"You trust the black man, Jake?" Broadus said.

"I think he'd have the confidence of the men if you assigned it, if that's what you mean. They respect a man, black, white, or in-between, who sees the errors of his ways and changes the way his stick floats. Now that John's no longer a Penn man, he's become a real man in their eyes, a mountain man."

"That's what we mean. You got John and you got Possum and Nate Chapman. We rule out Nate . . ."

"Yeah," Lyman said, thoughtfully.

"It'd be wrong sending Possum against Indians."

"Right again," Lyman said. "And I know John doesn't lack for guts. It took grit a few months back for him to stand up to Penn."

"Each of you take ten. That leaves us about ten, not counting me and Zeb here. We'll go up on the line and help fill the gap. Your man Possum has been reading the sign right along. He have any idea how many are out there?"

"We did talk after I went back. He puts their number at about ten higher than us. Not good odds, but I've been up against worse. Most of us that have ever gone up against Indians have."

Kern Abbott smiled. "You and John pick your ten each. Plan your moves, and go. From down here we'll see that the other sectors have a lot of lead laid into them."

"Thanks for picking me for this," Lyman said. "I've got a lot of scores to settle with our Mr. Penn. I'm sure this is the bunch that put Rene Lamartine under. I still feel some sore spots once in a while from the trouncing Simms and Labelle gave me, with Penn there egging them on. John and Possum took a lot of unnecessary and vile abuse from Penn for a lot of years. And they're fine men, not deserving of being used that way. Yeah, I'm ready to take Penn on. You damn betcha!"

"Then go after him, Jacob Lyman. Mind your topknot."

Lyman smiled. "Wagh, Kern, don't worry. Penn manages to surround himself with bullies—like Simms and Labelle. And I understand that sneak-killer Skull has lately been hanging out with him. You know him. About as fixed for hair as a boudin. Walk up and take a swing at that kind and they'll back off. It's come to a head and it's time to make a finish of it. I'll report back, you can depend on that."

"That Skull," Broadus said. "Ain't fit to shoot at when you need to unload your rifle and clean it."

Abbott agreed. "About as useless as a unstoppered powderhorn. Go sic 'em, Jake."

Lyman wheeled and strode off to find John. Jogging in a low crouch, he threw himself down where Possum, Nate, and John lay nearly side by side behind a huge log. There they had temporary safety from the hillside that frowned down on them with such a fury of bullets and arrows.

"Loadin' a Hawkins on your belly is pure hell," Nate bawled over the muzzle blasts of rifles around him, and the dull, answering reports from well-concealed ambushers.

Arrows arched in, visible but silent in flight. Bullets twanged past like vengeful bees. They were more to be feared. An arrow you could dodge, maybe. Get up and show yourself, and you'd never see or hear the galena pill that might sock into your hide. Now and then one of their blue whistlers would come chunking into the protective log. The sound always came after the bullet had past. So, Lyman figured, you never heard the one that got you.

"Paint for war," Lyman yelled, mostly at John, but so the others could hear. "Abbott and Broadus want John and me to take attack forces out of opposite sides of the camp. Show 'em some grit and maybe they'll skedaddle." A ball sang over the heads of the four of them, protected by their barricade.

Nate slid the Hawken barrel out over the log, his eyes keen on finding something likely to put a ball into. Lyman was pleased that Nate was in on this one; he'd been in the mountains a sight of years, long enough certainly to know how to use his tools. Nate paused, glanced at John and then at Lyman, a questioning in his eyes. Why hadn't he been picked?

"Con-demned stick leg," he muttered, answering his own question. Nate watched as a puff of smoke erupted from behind a tree a hundred yards up the hillside. "Iyeee, you con-demned idjit!" he shrieked, taking quick but careful aim, and firing. Lyman watched as a good-sized slab of thick bark from the pine hiding the enemy shooter skittered away, exposing a ragged circle of raw, white wood.

That sort of shooting at least ought to put the fear of harm into the besiegers up there. For some unknown reason, Lyman felt obliged to atone to Nate for taking John instead of him.

Possum had stayed silent, probably understanding why he hadn't been picked. His eyes, instead, were fixed on another sector over the sights of his rifle barrel aligned on the log. Something or someone had moved about twenty-five yards to the left of where Nate had just fired. The man up there just might be starting to get uneasy about the slick shooting from the trappers' camp.

"John," Lyman said. "Scoot on over to the other side." He was closest to John and studied his dark features. "By now the booshways have put out the word that some of us are going out of here after them. Splitting the attack force in two stands to reason. Break their ring and it'll collapse. If one of us fails, the other will divide them, and those down here can come up and fan out and make short work of the rest of them. Once we breach their line, it'll be plain old mountain-style

Indian fighting. No holds barred. Bitin', clawin', and chawin', even with the back teeth."

Lyman's eye measured the resistance on the hill as he talked. "Hidden like they are up there, they make poor targets. We've got to get in amongst 'em to get any work done. We may be outnumbered, but a show of plumb orneriness can always even the odds. That's what it's going to take to save our plews."

John pondered it. "Not so good, Jacob. Will those others go with a black man?"

"Abbott and Broadus respect you, and that's enough. So do the men. I've seen it, John. Don't fret—they'll go. It's all we've got."

"How many go with me?"

Lyman was pleased that John accepted the risky challenge that fast. "Ten from the other side. Grab the first you see, or hand pick 'em, I don't care. I'll give you a little time to get over there and get things lined up. We need a signal."

Nate Chapman's hand touched Lyman's arm. "Beggin' your pardon, mister mayor-domo. Ye may need men with two good legs, Jacob Lyman, but you crave some sound advice jes' now. I say let John go and round up his crew. Then pass a cease-fire order. Let'er stay quiet down here for five, maybe ten minutes. Like all of us had our lights put out to onct. That'll get 'em guessin' up there as to what's going on. Unsettlin' it'll be for 'em. Then I fire a signal shot, an' your two brigades go rippin' out like wild cats and extra lightnin' and send a few of them con-demned idjits hoppin' over the coals to hell."

Lyman grinned, his spirits rising with Nate's plan. Up to now it had all sounded like a suicide charge. Anxious excitement to be up and going filled him. He grinned again at Nate's weathered, old face. "I follow your line of reasoning, you con-demned old idjit."

A shout from Possum brought Lyman's attention to the

Indian. His head was nestling against his buttstock, taking a sight. "Jacob! Man, him!" Lyman's eyes swept the hillside to see the object of Possum's shout. A figure broke free of the cover of a huge rock, sprinting on an angle up the hill, probably to get out of range of the trappers' unerring fire.

"Simms, him," Possum said softly, intent on his sight-taking. His index finger stroked his forward trigger. The big rifle erupted with a plume of smoke and roar. Lyman watched the racing, rawboned figure on the hillside a hundred yards upslope suddenly break stride, dive like a man going for cover, somersault once and collapse amid the debris of sticks and pine needles, a jumble of arms and legs and body.

Possum had made a killing hit on his old associate, if that's who it was. Lyman, too, was certain it was Simms. Now, Lyman thought, let Abbott or Broadus make remarks about Possum's loyalty.

A cheer rose up from the other men along the line who had seen the shot. Lyman's spirits rose even more; first blood for Lamartine.

Possum looked to Lyman for acknowledgement. Lyman skidded over and thumped him on the back. "Better shot, by God, than mine on the grizzly, Possum! Look at that range! Damned clean shot!" Even though he was looking for congratulations from Lyman, Possum was nonetheless shy about it.

The shooting of Simms confirmed that Penn, after all, was behind this nasty business. At least one aspect of Lyman's quest was clear. From here on out his gunsights would be seeking Thomas Penn.

"Skookum! Good doin's, Jacob. Long, long Simms bad for Possum," the Indian said. "Possum medicine good this day. Wait long time. Before Simms do bad for Jacob. Long, long before. But Possum wait. Today chance come. Shoot for good friend Jacob. Shoot for long, long time Simms bad for Possum."

Lyman was exuberant. "You got even at last, Possum. You evened my score."

"Possum got even."

The Indian slid the rifle down off the log. He found a ball in his pouch and laid it in his right palm. With his teeth, he pulled out the short plug from his powder horn and barely covered the ball with black grains. Extracting the ball, he made a funnel of his fist and let the ebony explosive trickle down the rifle's tilted muzzle. He sozzled a patch cloth in his mouth, drenching it with spit. He patched the ball at the muzzle, pared the patching into a near-perfect circle with his knife, and persuaded the patched ball down the bore with his ramrod.

"Now Possum look for Labelle," he said, groping in his pouch for caps.

Lyman looked at John. "He's getting ready to take on that whole bunch out there himself."

John was philosophical. "He could do it."

Firing from the protected spots on the hillside turned sporadic. Maybe the word had passed that somebody from the trappers' camp had put out Simms' lights. "Good time to scramble over yonder and get organized, John," Lyman said.

John studied Lyman a long time. "If we get out of this, we better find us a jug this evenin', Jake Lyman. We gonna earn it."

"We'll find one," Lyman assured him. "Good hunting."

John looked at Lyman. "Well," he said, accepting ahead of time whatever the fates had in store in the next few minutes. "Hyar goes hoss and beaver!"

Lyman grinned again, feeling good with prospect of taking the initiative in the fight. "'Y gonies, John, you're commencing to sound like a winter-prime hivernant!"

Chapter Thirteen

The word was passed among the MacLaren men. When John's small brigade was ready to break out of the basin the trappers' guns would still. Chapman was certain that when no answering fire came from the embattled trappers, the brigand force would wonder what was going on. They'd become confused and slow their fire. In the ensuing stillness, when Nate fired his rifle, the skeleton forces under John and Lyman would counterattack "like wild cats and extra lightning."

Waiting, his racing heart sending pulsebeats of anticipation resounding through his neck and temples, Lyman knew John's force was ready when the trappers' guns in that area quieted. That was signal enough. Gradually, all the rifles along the trappers' line turned still. A waved signal passed from man to man behind their various forms of hasty protection in the sparse circle. There were grins as the sign moved along – and with it expressions of grit and good luck for the counterattack.

While John readied his force, Lyman had gone along the defense perimeter making his selection of ten tough fighters. They bunched close to him now, still pouring lead at the rocky, forested hillside towering over them.

Chapman looked intently at Lyman, maybe seeing his old friend for the last time, and spoke quietly. "Watch your backtrail up there, Jacob Lyman. No need to do somethin' foolish that'll undo your hairpins and cause your scalp to migrate to a coup stick."

Then the unearthly quiet settled in, in contrast to the rattle of conflict that had gone on before, a sensation heightened by the extreme cold. Not a breeze stirred, lending an ominous hush to the land. The silence all but rang in a man's ear. The attackers had to be wondering just what was amiss in the trapper's defensive circle. There was no way possible they could get any kind of word passed. Each man up there would have his own set of confused impressions. Even if Thomas Penn—or whoever was directing the raid—was holding a council of war with Skull and Labelle, there still wouldn't be time nor much of a way to inform his scattered besiegers.

In the awesome stillness, Lyman's grunt sounded like a shout. "Nate!" The old one-legged hivenant caught Lyman's eye. Lyman's mouth formed the word, "Ready!" Chapman grinned and nodded. Lyman filled with respect for the old campaigner; Nate was in his element. He was fit to fight. Nate poked his Hawken's barrel up over the log cautiously. One of the attackers, he knew, still lurked behind the big pine up the hill, the one with the white blaze mark where Nate's shot had nearly connected with flesh.

Nate cupped a hand to his mouth, loosing a high-pitched and ululating call like a turkey gobbler. A long-haired, beardless blond head abruptly poked from behind the tree inquisitively. In the same instant Nate's Hawken bucked with explosive authority and the head ducked out of sight.

"Con-demned sick old eyes!" Nate said. He'd missed again.

With the signal from Nate's rifle, a shriek went up at the opposite side of the camp. A surging excitement brought Jacob Lyman erect, his loaded Hawken extended over his head in the signal to charge. "Give 'em hell!" he screeched. In the same instant, a fierce war cry rose in his throat and as he started it, the other trappers picked for the charge bounced to their feet, taking up the call. "Eeeee-yoooh!" The stirring bellow was echoed by others in the hasty defense circle. The land around rang with the blood-chilling yell. Lyman leaped over the log, oblivious to exposing himself to fire, and sprinted for the hillside.

His command fanned out behind him, taking the slope at full tilt. Some of them came abreast of Lyman on either side, some passing him, others only slightly behind, but all hell-bent on one objective—to seek out and drive Penn's force off.

Now the roar of the fight picked up again in intensity. Bullets spat in the air around and over Lyman's head. As he raced toward the cover of woods that hid the attackers, he saw one of his trappers go down out of the corner of his eye. The French, he knew, had a phrase for it; "c'est la guerre." No one had expected they would get out of this without some casualties.

The determination and surprise of the counterattack by the outnumbered assault force had its desired effect. Lyman could see figures abandoning their selected cover of rocks and trees and bolting with hysterical frenzy. Near Lyman, to his left, a man who appeared to be an Indian broke from behind a rock and began a pell-mell route to some kind of safety farther to the left. Lyman skidded to an abrupt stop, suddenly conscious of his heaving lungs. He planted his feet, braced his body and raised the Hawken, his line of vision dropping naturally into the rifle's sights. The sights aligned at the base of the racing man's neck. The enemy wasn't making any evasive maneuvers to avoid being shot. He was running straight and scared, straight to wherever it was that would get him the hell out of there.

The rifle bucked against Lyman's shoulder. He suddenly thought that he hadn't heard the muzzle blast nor seen the smoke. In his excitement, he'd simply missed them.

His target spun around, legs buckling, and the man dropped into a dead heap. All around him, but at some distance, Lyman could hear the rifles of his small band popping. He hoped they were making their shots count. He dropped to the cover of a huge rock and swiftly reloaded.

Pausing to catch his breath, Lyman realized that though the attackers had the trappers outnumbered, they were spread almost as thin in their larger perimeter. On the opposite hill he could hear the sustained rifle fire as well, as John's small force made a good accounting of itself.

Behind him, the trappers still in the camp poured volley upon volley into the hills, careful not to fire into the areas of the dual breakthroughs.

Downslope from Lyman, a movement caught his eye, presenting a strange spectacle. It was the wounded Simms pulling himself erect on a rock, obviously aiming to find cover and some means—despite his wound—of making an escape.

The injury from Possum's rifle must have been a grave one. As Lyman watched from about fifty yards, Simms tried one step away from the rock and fell again.

For a long moment, Lyman clung to the protection of his rock, watching Simms below him. Though a small voice inside Lyman said to forget Simms and get on with the attack, a louder voice summoned him to wait. It would be a simple matter, he thought, to take one shot that would attend to the hated Simms once and for all. Still, admiration of the despised Simms welled up. Despite his wounds, Simms was trying to drag himself away with a fierce determination; like a beaver gnawing off a trapped foot. That louder voice also told him that the one thing Jake Lyman didn't do was kick a man when he was down.

On impulse, Lyman jumped up and raced for the badly wounded or dying man at the base of the rock. Coming near him, Lyman saw that Simms was gut-shot. Somehow he had pulled back his capote and reefed up the tail of his buckskin shirt to expose and inspect the hole in his side just above the waist.

As Lyman reached him, the rawboned man's dark-ringed eyes locked with Lyman's. In them Lyman saw not only hazy recognition, but also the pleading, the hurt that Lyman had often seen in wounded animals. And, as with a wounded animal, there was also a mindless sort of defiance.

Funny, Lyman thought, swiftly taking in the scene of the dying man sprawled before him. Men who were shot really didn't look all that different. There was that purplish and big puncture in the soft side of Simms' belly, oozing only a little blood. Lyman sensed that inside, plenty of blood was hemorrhaging around guts and organs that were pretty well shot to hell.

Aside from that awful, telltale bullet hole, Simms really didn't look that much different at first. But a closer look showed that the rigidness of death was already on him. There was that gritted set of the facial muscles, the disbelieving, surprised look in his eyes that he was dying, and the color draining fast from his skin, giving it a pallid, jaundiced appearance. A lot of men as they died, Lyman thought, really didn't seem to know pain.

Maybe, he thought, allowing himself these few moments to contemplate death as he got ready to haul Simms back to camp—maybe to die a little easier—maybe this was the blessing of death. Maybe that's when there wasn't any more pain. Lyman moved to scoop up the dying Simms.

Movement and crunching of twigs behind him brought Lyman alert to a new threat. He jerked around, suddenly aware that his own death was near. A beanpole of a boy charged him, on a mission of deadly intent, wild blond hair flailing around his head, brandishing a huge knife. The boy's fury and demonic determination were stamped in the purple of his contorted face. Lyman recognized him from the distance; it was the same boy Nate had fired at.

Startled into action, Lyman groped for his Hawken, set down for the task of lifting Simms. He swung it up, bracing for a telling shot from the hip. Something blurred in his mind; the raging, boyish enemy was almost upon him but something compelled Lyman to hold his shot.

Lyman felt himself abruptly filled with a strange sensation of recognition . . . through the eyes and the mouth . . . hard to come to grips with. His feeling of familiarity with this face was so strong he risked his life in moments of struggling to remember . . . . Had he seen this knife-wielding child before?

Where?

Rachel!

Yes! In the midst of the hysteria of combat, it came to him. A shriek rose in Lyman's throat.

"DANIEL ENGLAND!"

The charging youth recoiled as if shot, bewilderment and intense emotion searing his face. His pell-mell lunge at Lyman was stopped in mid-stride by the screamed name. The boy veered in his headlong flight for Lyman's blood; he spun and raced back up the hill, panic and stark recognition driving him to retreat.

"Daniel!" Lyman yelled hoarsely after him. His insides churned with a mixture of new and strange emotions. "Daniel!" Still the sprinting youngster retreated until he had disappeared into the network of trees uphill from Lyman and Simms.

Racked by the awful knowledge that he had at last confronted Rachel's long-lost son, and the animal he had found in him, Lyman dropped to his knees, trembling beside Simms. Lyman's confusion and emotional pain were all-consuming. Simms stared at him in these last moments of life. Lyman suddenly realized it had been a waste trying to save Simms. He'd be dead long before Lyman could get him back to the trappers' camp. He crouched close to his enemy.

"Who is he, Simms? Who's the boy?"

Simms made a tight kind of pained smile, exposing the ugly gap in his teeth.

"Orphan . . . Orphan. Skull's pet wolf. He's . . . the one'll get you, Lyman. Damned near did it . . . Orphan'll get you yet."

As his lips closed on the words, so did Simms' eyes. His body jerked convulsively several times, followed by tremors in the limbs and fingers. A new kind of peace settled in Simms' expression, and Lyman knew his old enemy was dead.

Lyman set his mind to listening to the now-silent woods, hunting with his eyes for any possible threat still lurking around the huge rocks and the clusters of trees scattered on the hillside above him.

Chapter Fourteen

The surprise counter-offensive, he thought, had its desired effect. Nothing moved. He heard the cry of a bird, shrill and nagging like an old woman, fluttering back after being rudely evicted by the din of the fight. As he abandoned Simms' body until he could arrange a burial, the land around him held a quiet softness. In the distance, uphill and off to the sides along the slopes, he could hear the intermittent popping of rifles. His team was either dislodging or killing off whatever resistance remained. Lyman felt a responsibility to cautiously check the hills, locate the men he had taken charge of, and get back to camp for a tally.

He picked his way through the silent woods around him, keeping an eye out for Daniel England. If he could see him again, he would try to capture the youth. His mind reckoned with the awfulness of it. The son of the gentle Rachel had become an ugly beast whose only passion was for blood. Skull, it seemed from Simms' last words, controlled the monster that Daniel England had become. Lyman also saw in his mind the day he would take that scoundrel Skull to account for what he had made of Daniel.

Trees sprang abundantly and randomly from the hillside ringing the basin of the trappers' camp. Almost as profuse were the great gray rocks that had peeled away and tumbled down from the sheer escarpments towering high above. Lyman cautiously scouted among the great and scaly-barked pines.

The fight had left his sector, as had the combatants, in the time Lyman had been involved in the aborted rescue of Simms and of the furious attack of Daniel England.

The massive silence that had descended over the slopes Lyman probed lent a false sense of security to his mission. All was quiet again among the trappers defending the basin below him. The sporadic sounds of rifle fire in the hills were so far off, or caroming from the opposite rim of the bowl-shaped basin, that they came soft and muted to Lyman's ear.

His gaze raked the surrounding land as he hiked the steep, needle-carpeted hillsides. Aside from the occasional, muted pops of rifle fire, Lyman was left alone to meditate on the attack and its shocking revelations. Still, he could not totally turn his mind over to the knowledge and the thoughts about young Daniel. Any one of these rocks or trees could still shield an enemy. Lyman made his way with difficulty, keeping close to cover in case a shot or movement should again warn him of a holdout or two still ready to lift trapper hair.

The cold breeze made itself known in this high place as a gentle soughing through the needles and slender branches of the leggy pines all around him. The sky was mostly open here, broken occasionally by pine tops, showing a rich azure with only a few puffs of stark-white cottonboles of clouds. Lyman shivered, partly from the cold, and partly from the awareness that less than an hour before these woods had been thronged by men who would gladly have taken his scalp to shake and show off and brag and dance over on this very night around the Penn campfires.

Penn's attackers had apparently been pushovers. Most of them, that is, Lyman thought. One or two could still be making a desperate last stand on this lulling, deceptive hillside. Penn, Lyman mused, could be providing a bounty for Western Fur Company scalps.

His rifle at the ready, Lyman guardedly approached a giant, gray squared-off bastion of granite as large as his cabin. Anything might be behind it; his nerves pricked to some unseen, unheard, unfelt danger. Maybe, he thought, he was being spooked by the amount of death he'd seen this day. His gun muzzle projecting ahead of him, he moved slowly and quietly along its side. Quicker than he could comprehend, a huge and dark hand emerged from behind the rock and wrested the gun barrel out of his grip.

Lyman struggled, but his hold on the rifle wasn't strong enough. The gun slipped from him and clattered away as the owner of the hand, a huge and nondescript Indian, his face ugly and scowling in the fury of his attack, stepped from behind the rock to confront Lyman. Lyman darted back a step to regain his balance and go for his sheath knife, his trusted and razor-sharp Green River.

Flight to save his skin was not on Lyman's mind. He moved to confront the Indian who towered over him. He apparently didn't have a rifle but was one of those who had been shooting Blackfoot-styled arrows into the trappers' camp. The Indian now faced Lyman with resolve, his own knife drawn.

As he crouched in a fighting position and moved toward his adversary, a strange thought crossed Lyman's mind. He had already thwarted one knife attack this day; such a fight must have been destined.

The Indian, too, hunched himself in a posture of knife-fighting competence, ready to sidestep the bite of Lyman's weapon, and at the same time making ready to stab or slash when Lyman moved close enough for contact.

Silently the two circled each other, eyes locked on each other's as though the eyes would somehow betray the enemy's next move. Both had become oblivious to everything around them. Each focused every fiber, every sense, every nerve on the importance of being first to make the mortal cut.

Slowly, like some strange ritual dance, they wheeled, drawing closer together, awaiting the moment when each would be near enough to strike. Despite the cold, Lyman felt sweat on his forehead and temples, trickling down his chest and dampening his crotch. His chest heaved in anticipation of the coming combat. As they warily took each other's measure in the circling maneuver, the Indian's cruelly twisted lips began to move. "This is a good day to die," he said in an Indian dialect, and in the fatalistic viewpoint common to Indians going into battle.

Lyman recognized the words as Blackfoot. He knew the language. "Then you've come to the right man for it," he responded in the Indian's tongue.

The Indian was a massive man, one who would not move lightly, his actions awkward, Lyman thought, assessing the tense situation. At last the Indian lunged. Lyman side-stepped, parrying the expected slash of the knife.

As Lyman leaped to one side, he heard the soft hiss of the Indian's blade as it sliced the air. Quickly the Indian brought himself under control. Lyman, too, caught his balance and leaped, straight at the Indian, trying to avoid the second cut of the knife. The Indian grunted as his footing twisted on some loose debris, chopping with the blade as he fell. Hurling himself at the falling enemy, Lyman caught the Indian's knife hand, getting a hug-hold around his neck. They rolled over on the ground, Lyman underneath the huge man now, locked in an angry embrace of death as Lyman struggled to cramp the Indian's swing. As he felt the weight and pressure bearing down on him, a suffocating kind of insane force and fury filled him. He wanted with all his might to be out from under the crushing, thrashing bulk.

Lyman wrenched himself on the ground. His feet found support in the gravel. Slowly he got his body tensed and, straining, bucked like a bullheaded mule. The Indian's body lifted enough for Lyman to bring a knee up forcefully into the Indian's groin.

The Indian exploded with a whooshing grunt that settled into a thin whine. Lyman gripped his knife with new urgency, brought it around and down, feeling it connect and skid and go on. The Indian flopped away from him and lay straining against the sudden pain, incapable of any more fight. The upper sleeve of the Indian's capote was ripped and going crimson-soppy with blood. Lyman burst to his feet, his right hand back, ready to stab again.

The Indian's fingers lay loose around the handle of his knife. For a moment, Lyman considered the knife thrust that would end it for his enemy. The Indian's eyes followed Lyman, sensing it was in the white man's mind to make an end of it. Lyman thought the eyes watching him were like those of some mortally wounded beast — like Simms' eyes. Lyman backed away, knowing he had won the fight.

Lyman stayed close enough to the beaten Indian to keep control, gritting his words into the kneeling man's ear in the Blackfoot dialect.

"If my enemy is finished fighting, I will not kill him but will attend to his wound."

The battered Indian bobbed his head in an angry affirmative, too furious to let words pass his lips.

"Throw aside the knife then."

The Indian did as he was bid, and Lyman motioned him to stand up.

"Pull the capote back that I may see your wound," Lyman said.

Beneath the thick blanket coat, the Indian wore a buckskin shirt that had also been ripped by the slash of Lyman's knife. As the Indian peeled back both to expose the wound, Lyman saw that around his neck, on a chain, dangled a large and ornate crucifix with a figure of the dying Jesus in high relief.

The suddenness of the recognition of the familiar object jarred Lyman like a rifle bullet. It had been at least three trapping seasons since he had last seen this same crucifix. He stepped closer to the Indian and rudely yanked it from his neck snapping the sturdy chain.

"Why you slimy son of a bitch!" he said. He flipped the cross in his hand to confirm the familiar initials engraved on the back in flourishing letters at the confluence of the two opposing members of the gold cross. "R.L."

The last time he had seen Rene Lamartine, the two of them bathed in a tree-shaded, deep eddy of the Green River after a boisterous and fun-filled "deboche" at rendezvous. Lamartine, euphoric from the gaiety of the annual frolic, had dived into the water minus everything but his crucifix, a token of his one-time devotion to his God.

The two of them had sported and shouted like playful kit beavers most of the afternoon, creating great waves and ripples in the otherwise placid hole, their exuberance taking the edge off a rendezvous-long deep glow of near-pure grain whiskey straight out of Taos. Lyman and Lamartine. They had even joked, whimsically, of forming a fur company if only to be able to use the alliterative name.

Lyman lifted the cross aloft in an angry fist, shaking it at the Indian.

"My brother!" he muttered. "My brother wore this. You killed by brother!" He and Rene had been brothers in spirit, and the term had the desired effect on the Indian. He averted his eyes in shame and acknowledgment of guilt, glancing sidewise, incapable of looking Lyman in the eye.

When Lyman spoke, it was more to himself; his words came out in Blackfoot. "I should kill you. An eye for an eye. But I'll spare you, you murderer of women and children. You sneak killer. At my camp you will tell me of Thomas Penn and how he pays you and others to kill from ambush. You will tell all, or I will cut these letters on this cross on your forehead. All will then know that Griz Killer Lyman has had revenge for the sneak killing of his brother, Lamartine."

Lyman again sensed movement up the hill from him. Startled out of his thoughts of Rene's death and his capture of Rene's killer, Lyman rudely shoved his Indian captive behind the cover of the massive square of rock that had hidden the man. Lyman held his captive near him, his knife deep enough in the folds of the capote that the Indian could feel its sharp tip in his side.

"It is a time for silence," he muttered "You won't have a chance to cry out, remember that. Griz Killer's heart will be good if he is given the chance to plunge his blade into your paunch!"

Again the Indian's head bobbed in assent.

A pair of trappers materialized out of the groves of pine, quartering warily down the hillside toward the flats and the Abbott-Broadus base camp. As they came, they walked guardedly, eyes scanning to the right and left and ahead of them.

They also looked back periodically for an ambush. In spite of his emotions of the last few minutes, Lyman grinned inwardly, observing their caution. Hivernants usually bade one another goodbye with the advice, "watch your backtrail." It wasn't idle platitude. In wilderness warfare, Lyman knew, being blindsided was more to be expected than a frontal assault—particularly if a man was alone.

Jules Bennett and the one Lyman only knew as Williams still held their rifles at the ready, crouching, ready to dive for cover if a shot was directed at them, as they moved easily around trees and rocks on their fast downhill angle toward where Lyman hunkered behind the rock's protective bulk and close to the ground with his wounded captive.

As they neared the rock, Lyman hailed them. "Williams! Bennett!" The pair recognized the familiar voice, and then the form as Lyman stood up and walked out to meet them, forcing the captive ahead of him. They relaxed their bent, guarded postures.

"Wagh!" Williams called as the two rushed to Lyman. "See, would ye, what Jacob found in his traps, Jules. A ringtailed, roarin' redhide! Ya only cut 'im in the shoulder, Jacob. Whyn't ya raise yer sights a mite higher? 'Long about the Adam's apple?"

"A man counts better coup this way," Lyman said jubilantly, still breathless and a-quiver from the combat and the revelation of finding Rene's murderer. For now he kept that information to himself. "Killin's easy. Hog-rasslin' 'em down and takin' the fight out of 'em's another thing. We need this one to find out what Penn's game is. I cut him bad. He won't die and I mean to save him." Lyman took the time to bind up the Indian's wounded shoulder. His knife had glanced off the collarbone and had severed chest muscles. The Indian's use of his left arm would probably be impaired.

As he worked, Williams and Bennett talked excitedly about the victory.

"Hyar's to the good scrap, Jacob," Bennett said. "We smoked 'em up for a fare-the-well. Comin' up hyar makin' more noise than a jackass in a tin barn done the trick."

"We hung up thar hides, and that's for certain, Jacob Lyman," Williams said. "I'm hyar to tell ye, them fellers has left these woods scratchin' gravel makin' far-apart tracks."

The three mountaineers, with Lyman shoving his unwilling captive ahead of him, began making their way down the hill to the camp.

"Guess I didn't get as far as you two did," Lyman said. "I got one. "He's layin' up the hill yonder. I went back, partway down, when I saw Simms trying to get up. Thought I might save him, but he died. I thought not much happened to me, but I killed one, fought and cut this one and was damned near in another knife fight before that. Say, you fellers didn't see him, did you? A towhead about seventeen tearing around through the woods?"

"Huh! Can't say as we did," Bennett said.

"Me neither," Williams said. "We covered a sight of ground too, Jacob. Some of them that went out with your partner got th'ough to us. We seen 'em, and they had driven off everybody 'tween hyar and there, though they said some of 'em fought like badgers."

"Likely if I hadn't tangled with this one," Lyman said, "he'd be doing his scalp dance over your hair along about suppertime."

"Don't you go to cashin' in our plews for us just yet, Jacob," Bennett said.

"Wa'n't much of a fight at that when you get right down to it," Williams said. "Most of 'em skedaddled like red ants out of a burnin' log."

"Goes to prove," Lyman said, "that they probably were on Thomas Penn's payroll. A man won't fight long for a cause he doesn't believe in. It was one thing for them to sit up here taking potshots from cover. When we came charging up the hill, most of them probably figured there wasn't enough money to get them to risk their scalps in a close-in fight."

"So it was Simms that Possum winged?" Jules Bennett asked.

"Yeah," Lyman said. "more than winged—gut-shot. Put out his lights. Shows that Penn was behind all this."

"Uncommon for Penn," Williams said. "He shines to odds a sight heavier in his favor."

"Depends on how good the money was," Lyman said. "He's on the take, that's for sure."

"Well, me and Willy figured Penn was around. There's a pard of old Simms that ain't going to be overly joyed to learn that old scallywag is headed down the chutes to the hot spot."

"What's that?" Lyman said.

"Well, we—that is, you—got this one hyar. They got at least one captive, too. Heerd John hisself got the drop on that Frenchie that runs with Simms and Penn and them. Labelle, ain't it? The one built like a high-cut hickory stump. I guess from what they got from his Labelle, Penn and his bunch has been campin' on our trail and coyotin' alcng behind us for a sight of time. Was them done it for Lamartine and some others."

Lyman's mind leaped. If they had Labelle alive, maybe he could find out more about his boy Simms referred to as Orphan. He wasn't certain he could coax much information out of the captured Indian, despite his threat to cut Rene Lamartine's initials in his forehead.

"Hy dang," Willy Williams said, still bubbling with fight and victory. "Surprised as a dog with his first porcupine, they was. So Penn may have got 'em worked up that liftin' MacLaren hair was going to be as easy as goin' to a church supper. When they come to find they wa'nt't but barkin' at a knot instead of the coon, and we come up here after 'em, them fellers had had enough."

As the three of them talked, more of Lyman's detachment began to appear at either side of them on the hillside, making their triumphant way back to camp.

Taking a quick nose-count, he hadn't lost a man. Even Larue, the one who he had seen fall on the way in, was on his feet. Relieved, Lyman greeted Larue warmly. "I took you for gone beaver a while back, Larue. Saw you go down just after we started up the hill."

"Slipped on the gawdam pine needles," Larue said sheepishly.

Chapter Fifteen

Kern Abbott's thin, fox-face gleamed jubilantly at Lyman across the blaze of firelight. Like Lyman and others in the camp, Kern Abbott had been at the jug. Around them, fires dotted the great sprawl of basin, and through the dark Lyman could hear the shouts, the murmurred talk and moving feet. Though the land took on a deeper chill with the death of the sun, the night sky cooperated with the festivities. Against a dazzle of stars winking in the cold of the everlasting firmament, Lyman could make out the bulking silhouettes of peaks and the black spear-tips of pines randomly poked at the sky around him.

The day's victory had sent the camp into a frenzy of jubilation. Thirty or so scalps still tight to their skulls was sufficient cause for celebration. The camp had the festive feel of rendezvous.

Say this for MacLaren, Lyman thought, he looked out for his men. Alex MacLaren was not given to loading his mules, outbound from St. Louis, with whiskey. Instead he sent south for a paralyzing potion known by many names, but best as Taos Lightnin', or simply "Touse." MacLaren's traders and *engagees* in the south also brought north about equal amounts of a Mexican conversation juice called aguardiente, which name came out of the mountain man's mouth as "awerdenty."

Trappers in other companies may have been restricted to a gill a day, but not MacLaren's, and tonight there was plenty for all. MacLaren had only one other rule about liquor. Flagrant abuse of his liberal policy, except for events like this night, was cause for banishment from the Western Fur Company brigades.

Over the chatter of a half-dozen clustered with Lyman and Abbott around their fire, the booshway's voice rose thick-tongued. "Make free with the jug, Jacob. You've earned it. Between you and John, they've taken to their heels. I've sent men out to check. Penn's humped himself to glory hallelujah, or I'm pore bull. He wun't be back. Guards are out in case he thinks he might like to try again. And, damn! We'll be ready for him this time!"

A dark vessel of aguardiente was handed to Lyman. Already he was feeling the heat of it driving off the cold that was fast settling on the land. With it came giddiness.

"You got Labelle and my Indian snubbed down good, Kern?"

"They wun't bust our hobbles. Tethered tight to the lodge-poles. And sober men on guard. We'll tickle 'em for their side of the story in the morning. Shove their elbows in their ears if need be to get them to open up. I just stopped by to share a cup with you, Jacob. Got to rustle myself and find Zeb. It shines for the rest of you to fandango, but Zeb and me's got a job of work to figure what's coming next. Thirty men, and gettin' 'em snug in the winterin' place gonna take a load of thought."

Lyman lifted the jug, feeling loose and at the same time powerful. He mimicked Nate Chapman. "Hyar's to the boosh-way, give him ease. Hyar's to mountain doin's, to do as we please."

"Ugh!" Abbott groaned as he heaved himself up from his log seat. "And hyar's to my last season, Jacob. Rheumatiz or the mountain man epizootic, one. Too many streams in freezin' water up to the puckerstring paralyzin' the privates before Mr. MacLaren made me and Zeb the booshways. Too many seasons so cold my gonads nigh fell off. No, Jacob, it's time to turn it over to you younger kits. Back to Saint Looey for these old bones. It's a decent house and a patch of ground and a hearth for me to parch my hocks up agin to drive out the miseries when they remember the beaver streams. Maybe even a woman to rub my joints when they commence to ache."

Abbott's eyes suddenly glazed with a faraway look.

Lyman's tongue was loose from aguardiente and he felt compelled to josh Abbott out of his dark mood. "Wagh, Kern. You're runnin' off at the mouth to hear your head rattle. You got a few more romps at rendezvous left in that old hide."

Abbott ignored Lyman. "And she'll be pretty as a fresh-painted wagon, Jacob. It's time to say good night."

Kern Abbott abruptly stretched himself to full height and shook his frame to loosen the kinks and cricks of premature age, jiggling the whangs on his hide coat. As he faded out of the brief light of the fire, walking resolutely, Abbott made one groggy sidestep, caught himself, trued up his course and disappeared.

From out of the night in the direction Abbott had gone, Lyman heard a whoop of recognition.

"Halloo, Kern! Dog bite me fer a bone if I didn't take ye fer a con-demned Injun!"

Abbott made no response as he weaved past a revelling Nate Chapman, who stumped into the light, eyes afire with celebration. Nate swung his pegleg around, planted his hands and plunked his butt awkwardly on the log lately vacated by Kern Abbott.

"Wagh, Jake!" he trumpeted, "hyar's fer Touse and fer mountain doin's! Fightin' MacLaren's fights do shine, they's so much fun afterwards. Happy as a kid pullin' a pup's ears, I am. Hyar's to Jake Lyman who presarved his scalp this day by tyin' it to his brains!" Nate clutched brown and gleaming potbellied jugs in both hands.

"Was wonderin' where you lit out to, Nate."

"Why roundin' the frolic fires, you con-demned idjit!" Nate said lustily. "Havin' a dollop and listenin' to 'em lie about what they done today. Where you should have been. 'Stead of sittin' hyar by the fire like a old bobtail chief waitin' on the war party to come home with scalps and stole hosses."

"I was fixing to hunt you up, Nate."

"Shore you was, shore you was. Sittin' hyar sippin' that Meskin maguey tea with booshway Mr. Abbott, you was. Thet awerdenty don't shine to Touse. Touse'll fix ye so ye can't hit the ground with your hat in three throws. Dogged if I didn't see Abbott out there in the dark reelin' like a pup huntin' a soft spot. Whoopee! This shore do shine! Old Possum, I seen him a while back. You got to l'arn him how to hold it, Jake. Old Abbott could stand some lessons, too. That pore red-hide already had too much an' is back there in the dark airin' his meatbag fer a fare-thee-well. A fare-thee-well! A good dose of Epsom salts tonight, if they was any to be had'd put him in fightin' trim in the mornin'. That's my medicine on that."

"You see John, Nate?"

"The onliest sober one in camp, by God! He personal catched old Labelle in his traps in the fight and he ain't takin' no chances losing him. Ain't a mite of love lost with them two, thet's plain as my rifle's got a hindsight. It's comical. John's perched by the fire in the booshways' lodge lookin' wise as a tree full of owls, holdin' a cocked Hawken on old Labelle, and a skull-cracker warhawk at his side if and that Injun you dragged in commences to git frisky."

Nate took a pull on one of his jugs before continuing.

"I poked my noggin in thar to have me a look-see at 'em. Labelle, he's keepin' mum as a clam with the lockjaw. I tried

137

to talk to that Injun of yore's, but he don't make sense even in his own lingo. I don't b'lieve the man'd know poop from wild honey, Jake."

"That Indian knows one thing, Nate."

"Which is?"

"What I'll do if he doesn't open up in the morning. I got the man that done it for Rene Lamartine." Lyman dug in his possibles poke, fumbling for the slick feel and hard geometry of Lamartine's crucifix. He hauled it out and dangled it for Nate to see. "He had the gall to be wearing this. It was Rene's."

"Put that geegaw away 'fore I get strick by lightnin'! I dasn't ought to cast a eye at them things, the life I've led. I'll tell ye soon enough in the mornin' if he was the one, Jake. All I got to do is look at his feet. These old eyes is dim, but they don't miss much. I seen the sign, you rec'llect, of them as put Rene under. If that Injun's track was amongst 'em, all I got to do is look at his feet and I'll know. Feet's the same as horse hoofs. Each one of 'em clear as the face of an old friend if you read the sign and mind what you see.

"Ye'll find, if ye yank off his mockersins, thet he has large great toes, and both second toes measure about the same len'th as his great toe, lumpy at the tip joint and I'd daresay with a thick nail. Both of 'em. Them's some of his uncommon marks, and he leaves trail lingo ye kin read like a book. Get 'im out of his britches and ye'll find a old hip wound around the right rear. Bullet er arrer. It don't give him a limp such as ye'd see right off, but he favors it ever so gently. A man with a game leg'll th'ow more weight on the bad one, depressin' it inta the ground deeper. If them's his sign, you got the man thet done it for Rene."

Lyman reflected. Nate Chapman was likely the best tracker the mountains had to offer.

"He done it, Nate," Lyman repeated. "Feet or no feet. That Indian got Lamartine."

"We'll know right enough in the mornin'. Just now we got jugs and they's more for us to jaw over."

All but two of the MacLaren trappers had left the fire. Nate eyed them thoughtfully. "O'Neal and Sayre. Hyar's a jug of good Touse. Whyn't you take it an' go whingding with Williams and Jules Bennett and them yander. L'arn yourselfs somethin' about hivernin'. Me and Mr. Lyman's got a heap of palaver this night. What I'm sayin' is—we need this fire."

Sayre and O'Neal looked at each other, pulled themselves up and took Nate's proferred jug and ambled away towards the dark.

"Much obliged, Mr. Chapman," Sayre said. He was young, still a pilgrim.

"Don't Mr. Chapman me, you con-demned idjit. Go swill the stuff, but mind you don't puke where I'm likely to step."

Nate studied Lyman after Sayre and O'Neal were out of hearing.

"They're good men, anyways, Jake. But it's their first season in them buckskins. Clothes don't make a man a hivernant."

Lyman was aware that much of Nate's bluster was for effect. When Nate got serious, his voice level changed along with his words.

"I did have my snoot in the jug this evenin', Jake. My sights was commencin' to double up on me. But it don't change my ears. I picked up a bit hyar an' thar."

Leave it to Nate Chapman, Lyman thought. He'd listen to the campfire chatter as he made his rounds and from it, if there was any grain at all in the chaff, Nate could separate it.

"You can get more from the hoss's mouth, Jake, but dogged if I didn't find out how the stick floats for our man Penn. He's a remittance man, they call 'em.

"A . . . what?"

"The black sheep, 'y God, of a family of nobility er some such. They's a Britisher crony of old MacLaren in camp.

Touring the West, ye might say. Goin' home, way I get it, and write a book about life in the old colonies. 'Special th' glorious American West. Book writers, hah! Jest like the rest of 'em, he'll get it all crosswise. But this one's a right enough sort. Reginald Brooks by name. The boys taken to calling him Chauncey, and he don't mind. Comes to the name now when he's called like a good dog. Chauncey knows all about Penn. Was surprised to run across him this close. Penn was sent off by the family and told never to come back. In return, they send Penn big money reg'lar."

"I'm damned," Lyman said, his head full of booze allowing him to be more than usually astonished.

"Penn's struck fire everywhere he went all his life, to hear Chauncey tell it. Penn got hisself in a scrape in Mother England and it come down to a duel. Trouble is the condemned idjit showed the stripe we know all too well and fired 'fore the other feller was ready. Backshot him dead. The dead feller's family and Penn's people settled the hash, agreein' that nothin' more would happen, if only Penn would hie hisself over the States and stay out of England."

"That explains a lot," Lyman said. "A man of his breeding in a country like this, sneaking around the way he does. This stuff against MacLaren. Commences to fit."

"Chauncey says Penn's been out of England eight years or so. He's been out hyar four year I know of. I'd wager he been tarred-and-feathered at least twice in the States and sneaked out of town in the dark five jumps ahead of the hangman as many times or more. Even out hyar he'll get his due when his due's due. Still a man's got to watch Penn. He's slicker'n calf slobber."

"English," Lyman said, thinking out loud. "Out to ruin MacLaren. You don't see the hand of the Hudson's Bay Company in this, do you?"

"Wagh, Jake. It don't shine. Their stick'd float for MacLaren and the rest to be east of the Missouri and have these rich beaver pickin's to theirselfs. Remember the business of old Ogden and the Americans? Hudson's Bay's McLoughlin's a decent-enough sort, but his man, Simpson, monkeyed around with Jed Smith, 'pears like after what he'd been th'ough, his troop sent under and losin' his goods in Californy. But I don't take them as high-handed enough to th'ow in with the likes of Penn. They's oneasiness in Oregon, but when McLoughlin's Hudson's Bay shoves, they'll shove like gentlemen. Canadian is English, just as much as if the land above the line was over the big water away from us. If they got Penn's stripe pegged in England, they can read his sign in Canada, too. Penn's reputation won't draw no letters of credit with McLoughlin and the Hudson's Bay. That's my medicine on that."

"And my medicine is that all this is bigger'n Penn, Nate. Penn's just the pan of the trap. Somebody a whole lot bigger'n him is the spring."

"You and me readin' the same sign, Jake."

"Things have gotten a lot clearer and easier this day, Nate. We know Penn's behind it. His claws were pulled today. Not likely he'll try any more bushwhacks of trappers out alone like Rene. That was the small pickings. This one today was his big grand play. Going to get it all done in one big yank and get MacLaren put under and pick up his money and git. Now he's finished with whoever's paying him once the word gets out."

"Likely we've dealt with that part of the job for MacLaren, Jake. Now we got to run Penn and them to earth and find out who's behind it so's MacLaren can go after 'em from the business side," Chapman said.

"In court . . . conspiracy, I think they call it. There's other reasons now to go after Penn."

"Which bein'?"

"Since we got back, there hasn't been the chance till now to talk to you. I saw Rachel's boy. Got to be him. He runs with Penn. Simms told me before he died. Skull . . ."

"Thet sneakin' con-demned idjit!"

"Skull's turned the boy into a killer wolf."

"No!"

"While I was up in there trying to get Simms down here to try to patch up, knowing he was dyin', the boy came at me with a knife. I saw his eyes. There was killer in them. Skull did the job right. Dammit!"

"How'd you know it was Rachel's boy?"

"Looks just like his mother. Age is about right. I yelled his name and it stopped him cold and he run off. It was Daniel, no question."

"Doggies, Jake! Wouldn't that gnarl a man's buckskins. What'll ye tell Rachel?"

"I'm thinking we'd ought to go after 'em, Nate. Right now. Before we winter up. Trail's the hottest now. I believe you could track 'em even after dark."

"Well, we was figurin' to split up soon's Abbott and Broadus and them break for their winterin' cache place. But I reckon Dawn Calf won't mind the wait 'nother week or two, if and it comes to that. It'll just make the goods that much dearer when I get 'round to 'em." Nate gave Jake a knowing wink.

Abruptly, Lyman's blood was up. "I don't think I even want to wait to look at that Indian's feet," he said. "I got all the evidence I need against him in this cross. Won't buy Rene back to learn the story from the Indian. Labelle isn't going to tell us much more than we already know, or can't get when we run Penn to earth."

"Wagh," Nate agreed. "That whole bunch of backshooters he hired ain't going to ride with him no more. They'll be scattered like the dust. Just hope Skull and the boy stay on ridin' with Penn."

"I'm depending on it. We go in the morning?"

"You want to talk about it with Possum and John?"

"Nah. They'll be ready too."

"Damn! If it was hot moon time, you could turn the Injun

and old Labelle loose nekkid and send 'em to hunt home whilst becomin' rich pickin's fer the gnats and bugs."

"I'll tell Kern and Zeb in the morning before we leave. They can decide what to do with the two of them, and make a report for MacLaren."

"Hyar's fer good doin's! We'll get old Penn and Skull down, 'y God, and paddle they ass! Then you can take that boy home to his maw. She, 'y God'll make 'im see the errors of his ways er I got your calico gal figured wrong, Jake."

"If only it's that easy." Lyman got up stretched himself to ease the cramps, and strolled away from the fire and Nate to find his sleeping place.

In the dark, rolled deep in his buffalo robe like a wooly worm wintering over in a coccoon, Lyman went to sleep picturing the four of them rousting out early after Penn . . . and Skull and Daniel England. Likely he'd have to put out Skull's lights to rescue the boy. But that was of no great concern; Skull had needed killing for a lot of years. Moreso now after what he'd made of Rachel's boy.

In these moments before sleep came, Lyman built grand mind pictures of getting Daniel out of Skull's clutches and jubilantly taking him home to Rachel. Awareness tapered off into the dark abyss of sleep and he slept the sleep of the dead, exhausted by the day's fight and his senses dulled by awerdenty and Nate Chapman's Touse. The night passed without dreams, without reckoning.

Chapter Sixteen

Soft light invaded the robe and worked around his eyelids, slowly urging Lyman out of the deep folds of sleep. Lying in a half-stupor, harkening to the camp beginning to stir, his senses told him the day was strangely rising with a warmth that had been lacking in the dawns of recent days. A good omen, his fuzzy thoughts told him. The chase after Penn and the rescue of Daniel might not be so impossible after all.

A voice and approaching footsteps brought him fully awake. It was John.

"Jacob. Been huntin' you."

Lyman thrust a touseled head out of his warm wrap. John's black face was wrinkled with concern.

"A good day to you, John. In case you haven't already talked with Nate, pack up. We're moving out after Penn."

"I saw Nate. He told me and Possum. But you'd better take time to talk to Labelle. Penn knows it was us saved Abbott's and Broadus's plews yesterday."

Lyman came fully awake and rolled out of the robe, sitting on it drowsily in the cold that radiated close to the ground, pausing a moment for all his joints and muscles to come awake. He coarsely massaged the sleep out of his face with open palms.

"I thought Labelle wasn't talking."

John grinned despite the urgency of his errand. "He is now. Nate and Mr. Broadus paid him a visit this morning. Asked him nice to open up. When he didn't, Mr. Broadus asked him how he'd like to be fixed so he couldn't tell nobody anything. Labelle just looked at him, all clammed up. Then Nathan went for his Green River and told Labelle to stick out his tongue or he'd go to pulling it out by the roots. Labelle started talking."

"Good for Nate."

"Penn knows it was us, Jacob. The kid with Skull, the one you think is Rachel's boy. He got back to Skull and told him about the peglegged man and the three of us—the white 'capitan grande,' and the black man and the Indian, all down here together shooting at him. Kid was half-wild—probably because you yelled his name at him. Skull got right to Penn. Penn now allows it's Griz Killer Lyman and the rest of us."

Lyman jumped up, shaking himself to get rid of cramped muscles and jammed his hat over his quickly finger-combed hair. "Let's go see Labelle."

Tossing the robe over his few stacked possibles, Lyman anticipated that the strong hot coffee he'd find in the booshways' lodge would effectively separate him from sleep, and grabbed his tin cup and sprinted after John.

The pleasant warmth in Abbott and Broadus' lodge radiated from a deep bed of coals and thin, jittery yellow tongues of flame in the fire ring. Like Indians, mountain men seldom built great, roaring fires. The same fire kept coffee grounds tossing merrily in a big pot of black soup dangling from the rod of the booshways' fire irons. Lyman helped himself to a cup of the nearly black stuff, feeling the fire of it searing the cup handle against his hooked finger.

An aroma that rose on tendrils of steam to meet his nostrils, prompted a pang of remembering waking up to morning at the cabin and Rachel's puttering and rattling around over the coffee and the whole place filling with these same smells. The pull rose strong in him to be back with her.

A hatless Labelle sat angrily and awkwardly on the lodge floor, his hands secured behind his back, a loop of stout rawhide around his neck like a thin and beadless Indian choker hanging slack but secured to a lodgepole. Like a great bear, Lyman's Indian was hogtied and lay silently across the lodge on his side, his eyes, burning in anger, taking in the action around him. His wound had been dressed and at least on that score, the Indian captive was on the mend.

"Good health to ye this mornin', Jacob Lyman," Nate said from his place near Labelle. It was good to see Nate looking chipper; boosted a man's spirits, Lyman thought. "I hope you ain't got the oneasy stomach from that awerdenty, hoss. But I 'llow you got a taste in your yap like you had supper with a coyote."

Zeb Broadus was also there, studying Lyman.

Lyman swallowed dryly; Nate was right. Still Lyman felt his gorge of aguardiente and Touse resting easily in his meatbag; it wasn't about to backfire on him. A tentative sip of the scalding coffee quickly rinsed his mouth of the bad taste.

"I'm fine, Nate. What's Labelle got to say?"

"Hear fer yourself. He's ready to yammer like a popinjay."

"What say, Labelle?"

Labelle regarded Lyman with suspicion. "If I tell you, Lyman, you will let me go, no?"

"Depends. Probably leave you with Abbott and Broadus for a few weeks to see how you behave. And give me time to track down your boss, Penn, first. Then we'll see. For the moment, you're safe."

"Monsieur Thomas, he very angry."

"Anybody gets 'is nuts twisted like Penn did yestiddy's bound to get on the peck, Frenchie," Nate said.

Labelle's eyes rested on Chapman, and swung back to Lyman.

146

"I don't care about Penn's feelings at the moment, Labelle. Who's behind this business of attacking MacLaren's trappers?"

"Labelle not know," the stocky Frenchman said.

"The hell you don't!" Nate said. "Answer the man or I'll fix you like I said."

A worried look crossed Labelle's face as though opening up with the truth was sure to get him killed. But he was shrewd enough to know how to duck the snare.

"Penn, he handle this business. I only work for him. Big man in New York—not Astor—but big man like Astor. Big *men*. Not one. They want control of fur. MacLaren, he big man in moun-tins with fur an' trade. Penn say put MacLaren under, make easy for him to take over MacLaren's business. Penn then be head man in furs and trade for New York men. Then drive out other fur companies."

Nate grunted. "Dog bite me for a bone!"

Lyman studied the old one-legged mountaineer. "That surprises you, Nate? We already had a pretty good idea of what Penn was up to."

"Runnin' it around in your head and makin' chin music over the fire and some Touse is one thing. We could of figured it lots of ways. Hearin' him sittin' there tellin' it straight and cold gives me the goose bumps. I'm partial to keepin' my ha'r, but I'd as leave walk up and hand it to a Blackfoot as I would to think it'd wind up hangin' on the shirts of the likes of the vermin that runs with Penn. That's the way their stick floats, killin' anybody that stands in the way. Naw, if I had my druthers, I b'lieve I'd cotton to knowin'—and respectin'—them as would bring in my hair. Eh-yah, it surprise me hearin' it f'om the hoss's mouth. Evil doin's, Jacob. Evil doin's, shore as my rifle's got a hind sight."

Labelle's eyes, still wide with apprehension over being a captive, darted up from Lyman to Chapman standing over him, and back again.

"You got any idea which way Penn is headed, Labelle?"

Labelle stayed silent, his eyes holding a distant look.

"I said, do you know which way Penn might be going?"

Labelle could no longer stand Lyman's intense stare and turned his head away. "No," he mumbled softly.

Nate, closest to Labelle, jumped behind the Frenchman and reefed his tied hands skyward, the unnatural flex of the arms crunching the shoulder joints. Labelle screamed a grunt of pain and bent his nose toward his knees as Nate's brutal hold doubled him over in agony.

"I got a feelin' that wa'n't the truth, Frenchy!"

"Labelle not know." His voice came strained with pain and muffled by his awkward position. Nate yanked again on Labelle's wrists, driving more agony into the stocky man's shoulders and chest.

"Penn is . . . he . . . go for Ly-man's woman."

Nate released Labelle's arms, but the captive stayed in his pain-racked crouch.

"Damn," Nate said, "if I oughtn't to open you from crotch fuzz to Adam's apple!" He looked at Lyman, fear growing in his weather-creased old features. "Jake, we better hightail it."

"Yeah. Maybe Penn thinks he knows where the cabin is . . . and Rachel. But don't be hasty, Nate. I know the way, Penn doesn't. He's only got a few hours head start on us at best, and he'll lose time licking his wounds from yesterday. Let's not go off from the half-cock notch."

Chapman's voice carried an edge. "Yo're takin' it powerful caz-yal. Penn's headed to get even with you th'ough yore little lady, and prob'ly work all kinds of evil on her and you actin' like it don't make no mind."

"Nate, Penn doesn't have any more idea where the cabin is than you do. You've never been there. Neither has he. Stop fretting. We'll catch up or shortcut him long before he gets there, or we'll be there in plenty of time to fort up before he ever finds the place. I'd rather catch him just short of the cabin than to have to march and guard prisoners for five, six days. Look at it that way."

"He could of sent scouts."

"Until yesterday, he didn't even know I—we—were in these parts. Walk easy. Heed your own advice. Don't get rattled and there's no way they can take your hair."

Chapman pulled himself up tall beside Labelle, still hunched over, allowing the pain in his shoulders to pass. "Well, if it's all the same to you, Mis-ter Lyman, I'm going to take John here and go roust out Possum and hustle myself down and look to our fixin's and get busy making up the packs and gettin' saddles on the hosses."

"All right. You go along. I'll be there directly. I've got some unfinished business with our Mr. Labelle—and maybe our Indian friend."

"Well, don't sit around here the forenoon sippin' awerdenty with Mr. Broadus. From all you've told me, I've developed a respect for that little calico waitin' at your cabin. I ain't about to see Penn get there before us."

"Neither am I. Just give me a few minutes."

"All right. But rustle yourself. Won't be more'n a moon I'll be watched for in my own lodge up with the Crows. I don't cotton to the notion of Dawn Calf thinkin' I've walked the long trail and get some spavined old chief that's seen his day comin' in sittin' on my robes in the west end of my lodge."

"Then go. Get started. I'll be right along."

Nate gave Lyman a look of wondering what could be more important than starting right out. He made as if to move out of the lodge. He stopped in front of the still-grovelling Labelle. Gingerly Nate balanced on one good leg and deftly stuck the tip of his peg-leg under Labelle's chin and lifted the pain-blanched face so it would look up into his.

"So long, Frenchy," Nate said. "See you in church—at your buryin'."

Labelle's head dropped again and Nate stumped out of the lodge. John followed him without a word.

"If you don't mind, Zeb," Lyman said to Broadus. "I'd like a word with Labelle in private."

"I've got to hunt up Kern anyway," Broadus said. "He was looking a little peaked this morning." Zeb Broadus followed Nate and John out of the lodge.

Lyman squatted close to Labelle. "All right. We haven't finished talking. I'm not going to treat you like Chapman did — as long as you tell me what I want to know."

"That Chap-man," Labelle said softly, his teeth still clenched lightly in pain. "He sommabeech."

"All depends on whose ox is gored, Labelle. It wasn't too long ago you had me by a fresh-shot arm, twisting it behind my back telling Simms to give me what-for. And how about pissing on my beaver sets?"

"Penn, he make me do it."

"Sure. But I'm not hanging around here to discuss who's the world's biggest son of a bitch. I want more information. What can you tell me about this boy with Skull? The one they call Orphan."

Labelle looked at man quizzically, as if wondering what business it was of his. His look suggested he figured the best thing to do was open up.

"From the day John shoot Penn, the day we nearly kill you, Thomas worse than ever before. At the fort, we stay a long time. Penn write lett-airs, wait long time. Make deal to put MacLaren un-der."

"All right. I know about that. What about Skull and the boy?"

"When we at fort, Skull come in with Or-phan. That all I know."

"Where'd the boy come from? In all this time, Skull must have told you something."

"Skull steal. Like horse. I think from Cheyenne. Or-phan

live long time with Cheyenne. Boy traded, but always with Cheyenne."

"Does Orphan know anything about who he was before he lived with the Cheyenne?"

"Or-phan know nothing. Only knows long time with Cheyenne."

"Has Orphan ever killed anyone?"

"May-be in fight yesterday. Not before. But he know how. Skull teach."

"I figured that. Just a couple more things, Labelle."

The Frenchman's head was up now, eyes searching Lyman's.

"The Indian there. You know him?"

"Buffalo Beard. Poor devil Blackfoot. Big bad man is Buffalo Beard. Blackfoot send him away. He that bad. He goes with Penn. Show Penn how to make killing MacLaren trappers look like Blackfoot."

"You must have been there. Was he the one that put Rene Lamartine under?"

"Labelle not know Lamartine."

"Buffalo Beard wore a chain around his neck with a cross on it. Where'd he get it?"

"Ahh! He take from killed trapp-air."

"You *were* there. Did Buffalo Beard kill the trapper who wore the chain?"

"Oui."

"You're sure. You didn't do it?"

"Non! Buffalo Beard."

"Tell me the truth, or I'll get Chapman back in here."

"Labelle tell the truth."

"One more question."

Labelle looked at him, waiting.

"Does Penn know where my cabin is?"

"Non. But he think he know where."

"All right, Labelle, That's all. I'll tell Abbott and Broadus to take you with them to the winter fort and turn you loose come spring. Don't come around hunting up Penn. I'm letting you off easy again. Let me catch you with Penn, and believe me, I *will* hamstring you next time."

"I think I happy if I nev-air see Griz-Killer again. I think Labelle go somewhere else. Back to Canada, mebbeso."

"That's the smartest thing you ever said, Labelle." Lyman grinned at the Frenchman as he lifted himself up from his crouch, picked up his tin cup and made his way out the lodge door.

Later, as he worked the tie-knots of a pack horse's load, Lyman's eyes narrowed in a squint against the glare of the sun getting ready to ride high in the sky. From his working place deep in their eight-horse string, Lyman just now couldn't see the mountains that ringed the camp.

Near him, deep in the work of saddling up and tightening cinches, Nate rammed his forehead stubbornly into the flank of a roan whose shaggy winter hair was stiff with dirt. Despite the urgency of getting started, packing up and saddling consumed just so much time.

Around them a new and fresh wind sawed at pine limbs, whipping them into a noisy frenzy. Uncommonly, it braced from the south, carrying a fresh, spring-like warmth. Snow, Lyman hoped, might hold off until they'd be able to get hot on the trail of Penn and what others of his band had stuck with the scheming and evil Englishman.

While the four of them were at work with the riding animals and the loads for the pack horses, the mischievous breezes made pack coverings snap and caused rope ends to slip out of busy hands.

"Con-demned wind," Nate muttered close to Lyman, his words muffled against the horse's side. Nate seemed to have to say something to temper the urgency that filled him. "They don't make winds like this back in the States. You got to come west of the Misery River to find wind. Regular old John Walloper winds. It's a wonderment, Jake, how come the percussion cap come along just when everybody was comin' out to wind country."

Chapman had finished saddling up, and stood back to study his work, making sure the job was done right. They might be on the trail till deep dark.

"Hell, I'd a sight druther have me a flinchlock in this country, but Old Squaw there in my fixin's is a caplock Hawkins, 'y damn, an' a good 'un. I hate thinkin' agin the day I run out of caps, caust I could always find flint to knap and be right peart to shoot agin.

"But, 'y God, wind like this'll play hell with a flinchlock. I mind the time the wind out hyar had a mind of its own to send the sparks skallyhootin' offen the frizzen and set the woods on fire 'fore they'd light your prime. And a man daresn't raise his frizzen in a high wind, neither. I seen the wind that'd clean the primer powder outten a pan and scour 'er shiny while it was at it. That's what wind'll do out hyar."

Nate seemed inclined to small talk this morning. Lyman, his mind on the prospect of getting started after Penn and finding Daniel, only half-listened. Their work done and ready to mount up, they stood talking, holding their reins.

Still, Lyman thought, Nate had to make his mouth go. His talk was bordering on being annoying.

"I mind the time I traveled with old Etienne Provost on the Santa Fe Trail—speakin' of powder—that we lost a blacksmith and at least a brace of pack mules and most of a wagon load of good tradin' stock."

Lyman looked at Nate, waiting for another of his tall stories. Nate sensed it.

"Naw, this hyar is fer fact, Jake. They signed on a blacksmith for the train to have a good man along the way to do the work on the animals and on the wagons. Thick-headed German or Swede, he was. Come one day they told him to break out a keg of powder caust everybody was runnin' low in their horns.

"He took him the only auger he had an' run him a little-bitty hole in the top head, picked it up to pour it into a bucket so's the hunters and guides and such could dipper out some and fill their horns. But it was a heavy cuss to hold up in the air, and the powder just come a trickle.

"So he cac'lated to open up that hole a bit. Grabbed him a hot poker outten his forge, thinkin' to burn 'er bigger. They said other than that, he'd be a tol'able blacksmith."

Chapter Seventeen

As the horses slogged up the forested slope, heads bobbing in rhythm with their gait, Nate's eyes were everywhere. Lyman watched him, knowing he was not so much alert to danger as he was searching for sign, quickly appraising every disturbance in the natural order of the land and making an assessment of it. Like a hound chasing a trail and then coming to full cry on a hot one, he led his trio of trappers directly to Penn's abandoned base camp.

Lyman's esteem of his old friend Chapman soared. The grizzled man's alert, bird-bright eyes scanned everything within their range from horseback, seeming to sweep in great arcs. His head imperceptibly nodded and swiveled as he studied each feature of the ground around him, each stone, each leaf, each twig. Every feature, every element within his vision was swiftly sifted and mentally catalogued. Its significance or insignificance was there to be called up and matched or discarded as he developed his patchwork quilt of evidence about who had been here, when, and what had taken place.

"The place is so tromped over, a man's hard put to be sure whose foot is which." he said, a tinge of impatience in his voice. "It's shore beaver though, that they went outten hyar ever' which way. The hull shebang of 'em didn't ride out together. His army's th'ough with Penn, thet's my medicine on that."

"Any idea which way they went, Nathan?" John asked.

Nate's eyes from horseback narrowed on the black man. "You mean Penn hisself, I take it. Look around you, son. We're gonna be lookin', I'd wager, for three sets of hoss tracks goin' outten hyar together. And pack animals. Penn, the rascal Skull, and thet boy. They's our game. None of the others of 'em count. Penn prolly never even paid them fellers as done his fightin' for 'im. Some of them'll be atter his skulp even more'n us. Lettin' 'em down the way he did. Jake, which way's your lodgin's f'om hyar?"

"Due east. Eight sleeps as best I can figure it, Nate, if a man rode hard."

Chapman's temper was short. "I only asked the d'rection."

Lyman figured it was time to be totally patient with Nate. A lot depended on the old trail runner. "Due east."

"Possum, you're a Injun that can track. You take Jake and ride a mite south by east, and loop back up north, movin' east. Me and John'll go north by east."

"Skookum," Possum said. "Good." Possum reflected pride in being singled out and the suggestion that, for the moment, he was superior to Jake Lyman and John. Lyman didn't argue the point. When it came to tracking, Nate was squarely the booshway. Lyman studied the Indian. If he had any after-effects from getting sick on Taos and awerdenty the night before, he didn't show it.

"Keep a sharp eye. Don't even blink. Mind they got pack animals, so you'll be looking for a least five animals makin' far-apart tracks. Though in this country they ain't likely to be at the gallop. But they'll be hurryin'."

From the tree and rock-studded hillside, Nate peered eastward as if trying to project his vision through the dense cover of giant rocks and thick trees.

He acted as if maybe if he stared hard enough, he'd see the

156

fleeing Penn, Skull and Daniel England and the route they'd taken in retreat.

"We ride up northward and bear back to the south, Nate?" John asked.

"Yah. Possum and Jake'll do the same from below us, to the south. Then swing north. Penn's got enough of a head start, and he's makin' tracks outten these woods, that it wun't hurt to shoot. Possum, if you and Jake strike sign, shoot once and then not any more. If by some 'tarnal evil, Penn's campin' on the trail ahead waitin' for us, there'll be a fair share of shootin'. Me and John'll come skallyhootin' in and take 'em from their hind side. If you hear shootin' up our way, Jake — 'cept for one round — you, 'y God, come a-runnin' painted for war. Either way, you come a-runnin', for me and John'll have found their sign."

Now that he was about it in fine fashion, Nate Chapman was pleased to be calling the moves. "Once we hit a hot trail — and we will — we'll figger then on how and when we run 'em down. Jake, Possum's going to be the eyes ahead on this one, watching for the sign. John, you do the lookin' back for me. It's as important to have a man mindin' the back trail as it is for the one scoutin' ahead. Protect your partner's blind side."

"Let's move, Nate," Lyman said.

"A couple hours ago, I was the one in the 'tarnal frenzy. Slow down, Jake, and let me think. No, I reckon I got it. The two bunches of us is gonna make like a big corkscrew, crossing north by east and south by east, loopin' up and loopin' down till we strike Penn's sign. Possum, you know the different sign for a pack hoss, or a ridin' hoss?"

"Pack horse him more load. Deep print."

"You got it. Count tracks, divide by hoofs, allow for work hosses and thet'll shore tell you how many men's in the saddle. When you're scoutin' the ridges, watch the flats below. If Penn's down there, likely he'll scare up birds, and you'll see 'em. I don't expect Penn's that close any more, but that sometimes can give a man shore sign. Penn and Skull, I'll wager, don't shine to coverin' the clear trail they'll lay. We'll be slidin' the groove come nightfall, or I'm pore bull. Okay, Jake, ride out."

Lyman urged his horse after the already eager Possum, prodding his mount downslope. Lyman tagged along, leading two of the pack horses and keeping wary for ambush from behind. Chapman and John disappeared into the thick trees upslope, eastward bound.

"Penn, Skull half day," Possum said, breaking a long silence ten minutes after the two parties had separated. As he spoke he waved his hand ahead, the direction they thought Penn had taken, and the time since they passed this way. "Okay talk while look for sign. Not much here. Jacob watch for strange stuff."

"Strange stuff?"

"Maybe broken branch, fresh scratch on rock, thing out of place."

"Shows they went through, eh?"

"Little things. Little things, Jacob. Watch out little things. Strange things, not supposed to be here. Then you good tracker like Nathan, him."

Lyman had tracked plenty, mostly game, but this was finer work. For him, it had never come down to a search for men. But he understood Possum. Men walking bent the grass in the direction they were going. Large animals, by virtue of their high step and dragging the paw or hoof back, bent it away from their direction of travel, he knew. But there was no grass here. He and Possum would have to be content looking for "little things."

There was, he thought, an entire science to the art of tracking and reading sign. He also know that Nate's reference to "slidin' the groove" meant they'd be hot on Penn's trail before the sun set.

Almost as he was thinking it, the corner of his back-searching eye flicked on something strange; something that didn't belong. The little things, by God, he thought. He was well past it. He reined up and double-checked it from horseback. Something back there clung to a low-growing twig. Out of place. That's what alerted him. Lyman's heart leaped. There was soul-satisfaction, he thought, when a man justified his own faith in himself.

"Possum!" he hissed, and the Indian wheeled his horse and rode back. "Unless my eyes are going back on me, that's a piece of buckskin whang fringe off somebody's britches stuck there." Lyman had better sense than to jump down and get it himself. There could be valuable sign around the site he wasn't aware of and which his blundering might destroy.

Possum spied it, too. "Skookum. Jacob no more Griz Killer. Possum now give you name Eagle Eye. Jacob see what Possum miss."

Holding his reins, Possum got down, studied the area and the article to memorize how low it hung on the small projecting branch. He picked it off, and held it gently in his fingers, studied it and smelled it.

"Cold. Long time here, him. Half-day. Good buckskin, him. Smell Penn. Land hard. No track. Possum think maybe horses come this way. Think for long time, but not sure. Nathan mad if wrong. Look for sign. Sure now. Horses go east. Head for flats. Easy ride. Head for flats. Jacob shoot rifle once. I guard. Then reload quick. Possum not so sure Penn that far ahead."

Lyman raised the Hawken skyward and discharged it with a throaty belch, his horse shying only slightly. The sound caromed around rocks and trees and the hills and rolled back to them more softly than when it left. Lyman levered out of the saddle and saw to his reloading.

Nate and John must have been bringing their probing loop southward, Lyman thought. A mere five minutes passed before the aging mountain man and John showed up through the thick trees of his and Possum's backtrail.

"Find ye suthin'?" Nate asked, eyes agleam with excitement. John was grinning. Possum took the initiative to report; Lyman wisely kept mum.

"Jacob see him buckskin piece on stick. Here. Cold trail, him. Piece from hide britches still cold from wet in morning. Maybe night. Penn far, far." Possum waved his arm in a sweeping arc eastward as he bent low to show Nate the twig. Then he raised up and handed the scrap of thin tan leather to him.

The old trail-wise mountain man studied it with the same intensity as Possum had, running it gently through his fingers and holding it up to his nose.

"Penn hisself, 'y God. Seam fringe. Huh! No mountaineer wears hide this rich. Good stuff. Like velvet. Smoke-tanned. Still smells, Possum. Soft smell. Not been around too many cookfires. Ner squaws. A man's nose can tell." Nate seemed to want to consult with Possum. For a moment Lyman thought it might be because the two of them had been left out of yesterday's counterattack. Then he realized it was because of Nate's respect for Possum's equal skill as a tracker.

"I take it he's come downslope from his high nest of yestiddy." Nate directed his comments at Possum, like two men going about a job of work.

"Huh!" Possum said in agreement. "Easy ride in flats. Penn, him always go easy way. Easy ride. Purty soon we see hot sign. Clear, like buffalo trail. In flats. Grass there. Horses bend. Good sign, him. Much quick, Nathan, we slidin' groove."

"Hoss," Nate said, "thanks to Jake hyar, we're already slidin' the groove. Damn! We got us two good men for this hyar trackin' fracas, Jake. Possum and John hyar. They've rode with Penn, know how he thinks. We've about got his hide laced to the dryin' frame a'ready!"

They rode out together this time, quartering downslope toward the tree-dotted basin sprawling below them. Nate had Possum take the lead, tracing the assumed trail of Penn and his companions. With John minding the backtrail, Nate and Lyman rode together, holding the lead-reins of the pack animals.

"I figger Penn thinks Labelle prolly bought his last ticket in the fight," Nate said. "That gives us a leg up, Frenchy spillin' the beans and all."

"If he thought we'd taken Labelle alive, wouldn't he worry that we'd be on his trail that much faster and with less delay because we'd know what direction he was headed?" Lyman asked.

"Money don't buy smart, hoss. Have you ever know'd Penn to do anythin' right? Even though we whupped his ass, he's prolly bragging to Skull on the clean getaway."

"I still think when we get on his trail, we ought to stay on it until he gets farther. Save the risk of looking after prisoners."

"They's still a better way, hoss."

Lyman stayed silent, giving Nate the lead.

"Wun't be no trick to steal the boy away from Skull. When they're in camp, the four of us'll keep a eye on 'em from the rimrock or the weeds. We're slick enough, they wun't sight hide ner ha'r. Skull's all Penn's got for woods-savvy, and Skull don't know sic 'em."

"We talked about that," Lyman said. "But steal the boy from under their noses?"

"Get the chance, hoss, and we will. Cotch the tadpole away from camp. Take 'im quiet, hogtie 'im—I calc'late he'll be about as easy to gentle as a greezed razorback pig—then hightail it for your digs, and your woman."

"And if Penn and Skull show up at my place, we'll deal with them when that happens." Lyman saw merit in the idea. "But they must be taken alive. Particularly Penn. He must be delivered to MacLaren to clear up who's behind this plot."

"Hoss, they might and they mightn't come after us to get the kid. With the kid gone, knowin' it's us that took 'im, Penn and Skull might just tuck tail and run once and for all. My medicine — and the sign reads the same — is that Penn's traveling with only Skull and your Daniel. Without the boy, and knowin' it's the four of us got him, Penn's likely to give up the ghost, as the preacher says."

"Two to one against him aren't Penn's favored odds. I say we try for the boy first by sneak. This way it's not likely there'll be a gun fight with Penn and a chance of him being hurt or worse. We'll corral the boy and then take up bringing Penn in alive."

"That's my medicine on the matter, too, hoss."

For the next four days, the trappers slid the groove on a hot trail, confident that their daily travels brought them closer to their quarry.

Chapter Eighteen

"We're close enough to smell 'em," Nate said, as sunset drove long shadows through the forested mountainside. "No fires, no shootin'. Gnaw jerkey. I'm bettin' before this night's out, we'll be helpin' ourselfs to Mr. Penn's vittles."

After eating lightly, they began the dark-time stalk of the Penn camp, each moving to a pre-arranged position.

Light through the trees outlined the forms of two men sitting close to a fire, talking quietly. In its feeble, flickering glow a plume of grey smoke spiraled skyward in the chill night air that was without wind. A third figure huddled in the cold some distance from the flames, obviously not welcome at its warmth. From his hiding place in the dark a few yards from the fire, Jacob Lyman studied the scene and made judgments. For some reason, Daniel England was made to sit away from Penn and Skull and was so cowed as to not build a fire to warm himself.

Even through the dark, Lyman was struck by how much the youngster favored his mother. There was no doubt. He had found Daniel England.

The approach of the four toward Penn's camp and their hiding places at the four points of the compass had been accomplished so skillfully that no alarm had been sounded. Crouching in the growing cold around him beside a thick tree, Lyman craned his neck, sticking out just enough of his head past the scaly bark for an eye to see. The plan was not to risk a confrontation and possible threat to young Daniel. Lyman had watched a long time already and was certain that Nate, Possum and John were in their places, watching like him, scant rods from the blaze that warmed Penn and Skull. With the cold moving from his extremities and into his body, Lyman already began to envy them the warmth . . . still his skin prickled in suspense.

Despite his closeness, Lyman was unable to make out the words of Penn and Skull; Daniel England only sat silently and sullenly, eyes brightly intent on the pair at the fire-light.

After an eternity of waiting, Lyman watched as Penn got up, shrugged and shook himself to work free the kinks of squatting by the fire.

Penn's voice came clearly now. "We'll be getting to sleep," he said, sounding like an order. "I mean for us to be up and moving before first light."

Skull looked up at this lord and master, but stayed in his crouch by the fire, making a grab for a jug that had stood between him and Penn. As Penn watched, Skull took a long swig, brought the jug down and waved it at the boy. "Here, Orphan. This help you sleep. Got big day in morning. Heap work." Lyman grimaced. Skull addressed the boy as though he was lower than any savage Indian.

Though he, himself, was no stranger to Taos Lightnin', Lyman felt a spurt of indignation that Skull encouraged Rachel's son this way. It ran through his mind that he'd have his day in at least trying to correct Skull's evil twisting of the young man.

Orphan pulled himself up like some obedient animal and slunk to Skull's side. He lifted the jug to draw deeply from its contents.

"I don't see why you waste good whiskey on the likes of

him," Lyman heard Penn say, as the big man observed the activity.

"It'll make a man of him," Skull said.

"The day you make a man of that miserable wretch," Penn said. The big Englishman fumbled with the fly-front of his fine tan-colored buckskin breeches and began walking heavily toward Lyman's hiding tree.

Abrubtly alerted, Lyman shrunk himself small in the dark behind it. Penn noisily crunched on leaves and twigs in the dark, veering slightly away from Lyman's position. From the other side of the tree, Lyman made out Penn's silhouette as he faced away from the fire and urinated into the dark.

A great expulsion of belly gas that accompanied it almost made Lyman grin. Penn hadn't the vaguest notion that his pee was nearly splattering Jacob Lyman. He knew that though close enough to touch Penn, he was nearly invisible. The dark, he knew, was darker to a man who had been peering into firelight for a long time.

Trudging back to the fire, Penn said, "Have the boy bring my bedding up close to the fire. It's going to be a long, cold night."

Skull waved, wordlessly passing the command Daniel had heard and understood. Dutifully Daniel went over to crouch at a pile of duffle and brought a heavy buffalo robe and some blankets nearer the fire and began spreading Penn's bed.

"When you get done, you can fix mine," Skull said. "Then get yourself to sleep."

Lyman grew even angrier at their treatment of Daniel. Squaw work—any man worth his salt made up his own bed.

After getting Skull's and Penn's beds made up, Daniel pulled a thin blanket from their possibles pile and headed back for the tree he had been propped against most of the evening. It was a bitter and hard place for the youngster to have to spend the night.

"By God," Lyman thought, "he'll sleep warmer than that when I get hold of him!"

Daniel tossed the blanket at the base of the tree and turned and looked at Skull in wordless quetion.

"All right," Skull called harshly. "Your're finished with your chores. Go and take your relief. But go on back a ways. Don't piss close to camp."

Lyman went rigid. This was it. The moment he and the others had anticipated. Daniel disappeared into the dark on a route nearly intersecting the positions of Nate and Possum. They had discussed it often enough in the two days before catching up with Penn's party. The moment was at hand.

Lyman crouched tensely, nerves twitching, muscles tight as iron. If all went according to plan, Nate and Possum were already on the move to confront the boy, muffle his mouth and drag him away. In the quiet, Lyman and John would slide back in easy retreat and the four would be on their way with their prize. Their horses were still packed or saddled and ready on the bluff overlooking the small basin of Penn's camp.

The quiet calm of the night air filled with a shrill and hysterical shriek. Nate or Possum hadn't been able to silence Daniel.

As Lyman's frame filled with the shock, he quickly calculated his next move as the lean and hairless man crouching by the fire dropped the jug and leaped to his feet. "Thomas!" Skull screamed, "We're attacked!"

From Lyman's right, in the dark sector that he knew cloaked John's presence, a long orange spurt and darting sparks of bright muzzle flash pierced the cold dark and the trees resounded with the Hawken's roar. It was the diversion they had talked of to keep Skull and Penn from going to Daniel's aid. John's shot was not for effective killing or wounding. They had insisted from the start that neither Skull nor Penn would be harmed needlessly. Both could provide important information on the MacLaren conspiracy.

The night that had been so quiet exploded with action. Lyman heard shouts in the direction Daniel had taken. Thomas Penn quickly disappeared into the dark on a line between John's position and where Daniel had gone. He was heading for their horses.

Lyman yelled, "Skull!"

A confused Skull pivoted and twisted as he tried to identify the center of action around him and the origin of the shouted voice. The bewilderment was too much for the sneak killer; scuffling where the boy had gone, shooting from another direction and now Lyman's hoarse call. He turned and sprinted into the dark after Penn.

"John!" Lyman bellered. "Their horses! Don't let them get to their horses!" Instead of crossing through the illumination of the fire at the campsite and make a target of himself, Lyman pulled farther back into the dark and fought his way through the dense growth to join John in the direction Penn and Skull had taken. John, he quickly thought, would be helpless in trying to stop the fleeing pair; he hadn't had time to reload and would be smart enough not to attack them with an empty rifle. In his mad dash to get to John's side, Lyman tripped on a root or a rock and pitched headlong, his rifle flopping away from him into the dark.

For precious seconds, Lyman collected his wits and fumbled in the dark for the familiar feel of his Hawken. He was aware of choked shouts, cursing, and much scuffling in the dark some distance from him. Skull and Penn, he thought, pulling himself up and starting again, must be at their horses.

One call rose distinctly through the dark. "Penn!" It was Skull. "The goddam nigger!" As Lyman neared the loud noises of Skull and Penn jumping to their horses, Lyman heard a bellow of pain. It sounded like John's voice. There were a few more yells and the startled beating of hooves. Lyman arrived at a small clearing where three horses were still tied to branches, shadowy lumps in the dark, bucking and straining at their tethers as the hoofbeats of the horses of Skull and Penn thundered away into the night.

Lyman quickly unloaded his rifle in the direction of their panicked flight, and swore.

What appeared to be the body of a man lay near the horses. Lyman quickly knelt over him.

"John! John!" he called. He ran his hands over the unconscious body. Quickly he grabbed one arm and a leg and heaved John to his shoulders and started back to the fire. "Nate!" he bellowed, his lungs heaving, his breath coming in gasps. "Possum!"

"We're all right." He heard Nate's distant voice out of the night. "We got 'im!"

Quickly as he could, loaded as he was, Lyman again fought the tangled undergrowth as he struggled to get back to the fire. He waded quickly back into its light, certain now it was safe. Skull and Penn had escaped, and wouldn't be back.

Gently, tenderly he eased John's body down to the thick bedding that had been intended for Thomas Penn. Nate and Possum appeared in the waning firelight, shoving the unwilling Daniel England ahead of them, fighting, snarling, and kicking.

"We gotta get this 'un snubbed down, Jake!" Nate yelled. Each of them held one of Daniel's arms, trying at the same time to carry their Hawkens and avoid the young man's hysterically flailing legs and feet.

"Do it," Lyman commanded loudly. "John's been hurt."

Nate and Possum dragged young Daniel closer to Lyman crouching over John's body. Lyman took a moment to toss some sticks on the glowing coals to get enough light to see by.

"He's been hurt bad." As the light flared up, Lyman could see that John's head was a bloody mess, his tight, kinky mat of black hair glistening with carmine blood. Blood, he suddenly thought, seemed even redder in contrast against the jet-

168

black hair and ebony skin of a black man. As the flames quickly leaped higher, he saw two great red-flowing lacerations running from John's temple and up toward the top of his head.

As John had moved to stop Skull and Penn, one of them—probably Skull—must have jabbed at him with the iron crescent of the rifle's butt, the two metal points carving the deep wounds. John groaned and Lyman's heart soared. His friend was still alive.

"They laid his head open," he said to the pair who stood across the fire contending with the struggling Daniel "He'll be all right. Likely we'll have to sew him up."

"Best do it while he's still out," Nate said, his words labored as he struggled to control Daniel. "Try it after he wakes up and ya'll hafta knock him cold again to stop his squirmin'."

"Got thin sinew, little needle in possibles on horse," Possum said. He grunted as Daniel, in an insane fury, fought again to get away from the iron grip of the old trapper and the Indian.

"Possum," Nate said, "Where's some rope or thong. Let's get this 'un gentled."

"Possum hold Daniel, him." Clutching Daniel's arm, Possum stepped behind the boy, relieved Nate of the arm he held and securely pinioned Daniel's arms behind him. "Nathan him hunt rope." The boy tried to fight Possum's grip, which was now even more effective than when the two of them held him from the sides. Try as he might, Daniel England was going nowhere this night.

Nate stumped to the stack of possibles left by Skull and Penn. "Hyar's enough wove rawhide rope to hold him till the Kingdom comes." With it he and Possum secured the furious young Daniel while Lyman got a blanket over John and dribbled some of Skull's Taos Lightning over the wounds.

"Good medicine, Jake," Nate commented as he fixed the last of the knots on Daniel's hands and feet. He watched Lyman drip whiskey over John's wounds to cleanse them. "Thet buttplate thet been up to Skull's shoulder for all his backshootin' has enough boogers on it to mortify the wounds of a army. We got this chil' snubbed down good, Possum. Let's go fetch down the hosses and find that sinew and get ol' John's head sewed up."

Lyman stood up, content that he had done as much for John as he could for the moment. "Good," he said. "I'll watch Daniel till you get back."

"Keep a eye shinin' for Skull. A man like him don't favor gettin' his pet wolf and his camp kicker stole from him," Nate said. "The con-demned idjit's likely to come ridin' back in hyar orn'rier than a hive of homeless hornets."

Lyman looked at Nate, sensing victory. "We did it. We got him."

"Yah, hoss, we got 'im," Nate said philosophically. "But look at 'im. It's a mis'able git we got. He'll need a scrubbin' and clean fixin's 'fore he's fit to ride with us. I know I ain't that partial to bathin', but this 'un's considerably whiffy upwind or down."

"All in good time, Nate," Lyman said. "All in good time."

As Nate and Possum disappeared into the dark, moving quietly and warily, Lyman took one last look at John, satisfied that he was resting comfortably and soon would have the long but shallow lacerations closed. He walked around the fire to where Daniel England lay on his side, eyes flashing, his legs drawn up behind his back, his ankles tied close to his wrists.

"So you're the one they call Orphan," he said. "Do you remember trying to kill me with a knife in the big fight? I called your name, and you ran away. You're not Orphan any more. From now on get used to the name of Daniel England."

The youngster mumbled something unintelligible to Lyman.

"Do you remember coming out from the east in a wagon train with your father and mother?"

Still the eyes flashed out of the grimy face and Daniel clamped his jaw tighter.

"You were carried off by the Cheyenne. That's where you've lived for more than five years. Skull stole you from them. Your father was Edwin England, an Army officer killed the day you were captured. Your mother's name is Rachel. I'm going to take you to her."

Daniel made his mouth move but only murmurring sounds came out.

"Are you trying to tell me something?"

The boy scowled up at Lyman, biting his lip. He glared at Lyman a long time.

"Aim gah mo muvver," Daniel said.

"At least you're talking to me, but I can't make head nor tails of that."

The boy glared again and repeated the strange-sounding words.

Lyman rolled the words around in his head. It was no Indian dialect he'd ever heard and it surely wasn't English. He tried to repeat the words mentally, slowly and then fast. "Aim gah mo movver . . ." The light dawned on his brain.

"I got it. You just said you ain't got no mother."

The boy nodded sullenly and Lyman sensed a thrill that he was getting through to him. Again Daniel repeated it, but with less anger. "Aim gah mo muvver."

Lyman spirits soared. "Oh, yes, you do, son. You've got a mother named Rachel. She's waiting for you, not far from here."

"Mo muvver. Skull favver. Love Skull. Where Skull?"

Lyman's heart sank.

"My God, boy," he said. "What have they done to you?"

Chapter Nineteen

In the morning after they had eaten, Nate Chapman sat by the breakfast fire, idly poking at it with a long stick.

"No point in taking the boy home to his maw in his condition, Jake. He's got to be scrubbed. Any river's too condemned cold to get in there with him long enough to give him a sure-enough dousin'. I'd say jes' th'ow him in, but that'd just make him madder'n a wet cat, when what we're tryin' to do is gentle 'im. Ain't no hot springs hereabouts neither. That'd shine, if and we could find one."

"Taking him home's going to be bad enough after what he's become, Nate. I don't know what we can do about that, just now. Going to take time. But we sure got to clean him up, if there's a way. Heat a bunch of water, I suppose."

"They's a easier way, hoss."

"Which is?"

"Build us a sweat lodge. Penn's left enough robes and blankets with what we got. They's a sight of willer shoots for a frame, and Lord knows enough rocks to heat for the steam. Then run him down to that cold crick yander and baptize 'im an' I'll wager he'll be cleaner in his head as well as in 'is hide. Ain't one of us but could stand a good sweat after he's cooked and cooled. Us four could go first, jus' to show 'im there's no harm comin' to 'im."

"Might as well. Last night's fracas bought us a little time. I believe Penn will give up the idea of trying to find my cabin, at least for now."

Chapman gave Jake an agreeing grin. "Him and Skull's skedaddled with their shirt tails out to the cold and their britches don't cover their hind ends. Like ol' Labelle, Penn just now is probably hopin' he's seed the last of Griz Killer and ol' Stick Leg and John and Possum."

Lyman grinned back. "But don't count on it. He'll be back to get even in his own good time and in his own evil way. I just hope we're not misjudging him by not making tracks to get home and protect Rachel." Lyman let it drop there; Penn could never find his cabin. He'd hidden it too well. "So, a sweat lodge it is. We'll need to chop off some of Daniel's hair, too. Trim it back to his collar, anyway."

"Could do it with a knife, but I'd wager our Mr. Penn's got him some shears there in his plunder. Make it a sight easier and a sight better job." Nate motioned at two stiff rawhide boxes or parfleches the size of small trunks. They were richly decorated, Indian-style, with reds, blues and greens of plant and earth dyes in eye-pleasing patterns. The thick rawhide was almost as tough as iron, and infinitely lighter.

"Hey, Possum," Nate called. "Go nose around in them parfleches. We needin' some scissors." He held up a hand and made a cutting sign with two fingers. "See if they ain't some buckskins in thar, too. We got to burn them togs Dan'l's got on, less'n we need somethin' gawdaful sour-smellin' to spook the wolves."

"Burn 'em," Lyman said.

"Wouldn't hurt none of us to clean up 'fore we get to your digs, Jake. Respect for your little calico, and all. She's going to have enough on her hands seein' her chil' this way, 'thout a gang of whiffy mountaineers lollygaggin' around. You in particular, Mr. Jacob Lyman. And shave some whiskers. The lad learnt one good thing with the Cheyenne. Looks like he tweezered 'em out with leetle clamshells as they sprouted. Wisht I'd of done that. Too late now. Come snow, though, it's a comfort to have a face full of fur."

Lyman studied Nate and nodded in agreement.

Possum trudged to the stack of duffle left by Penn and Skull, opened the parfleches and began rummaging through Penn's possibles in his search for scissors and clothing for Daniel.

"Let's roust ourselfs and get to cuttin' some switches for the frame, Jake. Clean everybody up and be on our way. I still ain't going to rest easy till I see your little woman safe and sound," Chapman said.

Lyman jumped up, working his knife free, eager to get started. The cabin was but an easy two-day ride. That close, the pull to be home rose up strong in him.

John emerged out of the thickets where he had gone to squat after a full breakfast and hot coffee. His hat covered last night's stitching of his wounds from the butt of Skull's rifle. Aside from that healing process, Lyman thought, John was making a satisfactory recovery despite what John had said was a "larrupin'" headache.

"John!" Lyman called. "We're going to build a sweat lodge. Pull together all the robes and blankets and start hunting the right rocks. Nate and I'll see to the framing."

John grinned, showing two white rows of well-placed teeth that gleamed brighter against his coffee-colored skin. He waved a salute of agreement. No, Lyman thought, there was nothing wrong with John that a few days wouldn't mend. Lyman started after Nate.

He was stopped by Possum's call from the heap of belongings he had pulled from the rawhide boxes. He waved a pair of shears. "Jacob, Nathan! Britches him, shirts. Good moccasins. More, Jacob, more. Penn white man's talking leaves."

Lyman looked quizzically at Nate, standing near him.

"Letters, hoss. Penn's papers."

Lyman leaped to where Possum stood over the piles of things he had dug out. Possum knelt and produced two bulging packets of documents, some of them in thick paper wallets, all secured with narrow buckskin thongs.

Possum handed them to Lyman; the others crowded around.

"I'm thinkin' you'll prob'ly find in there what you need to send off to MacLaren, Jake," Nate said, sober as a judge pronouncing sentence, peering at the bundles over Lyman's shoulder.

Lyman undid one of them and opened the three-way fold of a letter dated months before in New York. It showed the fine writing hand of a confidential clerk or some such and was on quality letter paper. The formalities of the words and the fine flair and flourishes of the pen seemed to Lyman oddly out of context in this primitive wilderness.

He scanned the first letter quickly, his eyes only briefly fixing on significant words, and then unfolded the next. There would be plenty of time later on for careful reading. What was even more sinister were names, dates, and details of the heinous proposal.

Nate Chapman was right. Now they had the evidence that fully incriminated Thomas Penn in a conspiracy to destroy MacLaren's Western Fur Company. There it was in black and white.

He felt his insides swell with a great surge of pride in accomplishment. Penn's fangs were effectively pulled, if they hadn't been by the fight at the Abbott and Broadus camp. These papers represented the final nail in the coffin of Mr. Thomas Penn. Rene Lamartine's death, at last, was atoned.

Beside Lyman, Possum craned his neck to look at the quill scratching on the paper; they were as meaningless to him as Egyptian hieroglyphics. Lyman held the bundles of letters in his left hand and shoved his right at Possum for a shake. Possum took his hand, looking bewildered, but pumping Lyman's arm in a solemn, Indian-type protocol.

"Good hunting, Possum. Penn won't ever again use anyone the way he used you and John, and Skull won't ever again bedevil young Daniel there."

Lyman swung a thoughtful eye at the hogtied figure by the fire, the glint of his eyes sullenly following the activity around Penn's open and empty parfleches. Everything for Lyman had suddenly fallen into place. Almost everything, he thought. There remained only one thorn in his side; the animal Daniel England had become. What kind of a prize was he taking home to Rachel?

Things, Lyman thought, might begin to right themselves when they were able to get Daniel cleaned up. That was the next step.

John also hung close, standing beside Possum for a look at the damning evidence against Penn. Lyman retied the thongs around the one bundle he had opened.

"Here, John," he said, handing the packages to him. "You take care of these. Guard them. Read them — all of us should who can read. It'll make these last few months worthwhile." He looked into the eyes of Possum and Nate. "Dumb as it sounds, we've got to take an oath amongst us that no matter what happens, one of us will get these papers to MacLaren."

The eyes of the three were suddenly on him. "Thomas Penn's a proud man," Lyman continued, "and a desperate man. That's a bad combination. He doesn't take defeat lightly. He'll try, if he can figure a weasel's scheme, to get these letters back. He wouldn't for a minute hesitate to kill any and all of us for them."

"Straight medicine, hoss," Nate said soberly. "Only hope Penn ain't headed straight for your cabin."

That worry was strong in Lyman, too. "Are we agreed?" he said.

Possum grunted in understanding. John looked into Lyman's eyes and nodded. Lyman felt Nate's hand on his shoulder. "I was the one found young Lamartine dead, you rec'llect. You know how my stick floats."

"Done," John said. "What we waitin' for? We got us a sweat lodge to build."

"How's your head, John?" Lyman asked.

"Apart from feelin' like it's about to crack open and let the innards spill out, I reckon about as well as can be expected." A broad grin split his face.

"You remember nursemaiding me after Simms and Labelle lodgepoled me for a fare-thee-well? I know what you're going through."

John grinned at him again. "You lived through it. We both got hard heads. If you made it, so will I. A sweat lodge cure ought to about put me on my feet."

"You fellows get busy on it," Lyman said. "Let me trim young Daniel's hair. I need to get him accustomed to me."

Possum handed the shears to Lyman and the three of them got busy with the chore of setting up the hasty steam chamber. They'd fashion a small dome-like structure of willow shoots stuck in the ground, and then bent and tied together at the center. Over this they'd spread and stake the buffalo robes and blankets to effectively keep any the steam inside.

Rocks were heated clear through in the fire. They'd be carefully packed into the lodge's small circular space. Just before the patient entered, the mountaineers would douse the hot rocks with water to produce thick steamy vapors. A man would sit nude in the moist, hot air about as long he could stand it, then make a dash for the river, and dunk himself for an instant in its iciness. As Nate said, a sweat lodge and the icy plunge had a way of cleaning up the head as well as the hide, and the heart and the soul, not to mention muscles and joints.

Lyman approached Daniel with the scissors. The young man was still hog-tied. Lyman spoke in a calming voice, as he might to a skittish horse. "Now, son, I want you to hold yourself still. We got to get some of that hair off before you go to see your mother."

He lifted a handful of the greasy, smelly hair alongside Daniel's head and held it up, showing him the scissors. "Now if you don't jump around, things will go okay. You start thrashing and I don't know that I might chop off a bit of ear, or worse.

"Neave hair alome," Daniel grunted.

"Oh, no. You're going to get it cut and get cleaned up and into some new clothes whether you like it or not. How'd you like to sit up?" He helped Daniel into a kneeling position, his heels out behind him, his hands thrust down behind his back, tied as they were by the wrists close to his ankles. Lyman tried to be gentle.

"That's good," Lyman said. He still approached Daniel gingerly. "If I could trust you not to try to make off, I'd untie you. We're your friends, boy. You're in no danger with us, and we won't mistreat you like Skull did. But you're a long way from believing that. Now just hold still."

Suddenly there was in the boy a quick but strange acceptance.

"Orphan always prisoner. Orphan be good."

"With us you're only a prisoner because you will it that way. You could be free as a bird if you'd behave. Just now I want you to hold still. It'll sure help."

Lyman grasped the long hair again and brought the shears to bear and lopped off a great handful. By slow degrees he worked around the young man's head, trimming the greasy blond hair to collar length and short around the ears.

It would look better, he thought, if he were able to shape it with his sharp knife. After he had hacked away the worst of it with the shears, he tried the knife, pleasing himself with the results of his work.

Nate wandered past to admire Daniel's new looks. "Dogged if it don't look like you're findin' a human critter underneath all that thatch, Jake."

Daniel held his head steady, tipped down to allow Lyman to work. He rolled his eyes up to regard Nate's grin sullenly.

"Loosen up, boy," Chapman said. "We's friends, me and Jacob."

Nate moved as if to pat the boy good-naturedly on the cheek. Daniel shied, and Lyman jerked the knife away to avoid cutting him.

"I don't believe he's ready to be joshed with."

Nate was clearly displeased with Daniel's reaction. "He'll change 'is tune when he comes face to face with 'is mother. She wun't put up with 'is muleyness."

"We're doing fine here, Nate. Go get the sweat lodge up."

"A good sweat'll help his disposition," Nate said, getting in the final word.

It was late morning before the lodge was ready, and Nate and John took the first turn. Nate took off everything including his pegleg, using a stout stick as a crutch. His head, neck and hands were nearly as brown as John's; by contrast, his body was white as pearl. Before going into the lodge, Nate and John turned their clothes inside out to air.

"You wun't find ary lice ner nits in them skins of mine," Nate said. "Ever I find the seam-squirrels comin' into them things to live with me, I take 'em off and spread 'em near a anthill. Ants'll make short work of vermin an' sech critters."

After Lyman and Possum had their turn, the four of them, naked as jaybirds despite the chilly mid-day, got Daniel out of his smelly, threadbare and worn clothing. Forcibly escorting him to the lodge, they stood by while he unwillingly occupied the structure for more than a quarter-hour. Amid great glee, Lyman, Possum and John propelled him to the nearby stream for a chilling dip. Fierce at first, Daniel seemed to mellow during the march back to camp as his blood began to circulate warmly through his clean skin and well-steamed and then thoroughly chilled muscles.

At camp, Nate had dressed himself and laid out a pair of moccasins, a calico shirt belonging to Penn, and a set of Skull's buckskin breeches. The abandoned parfleches also yielded up a short-skirted coat of thick Hudsons Bay blanketing material; it appeared to be a cut-down capote. Lyman's broad beaver hat offered enough protection, he thought, so he topped Daniel's new outfit with his own fur cap.

The four of them clustered around Daniel as he dressed, making sure he didn't try to get away. John stood back and studied the boy.

"Dan," he said, using the nickname for the first time, "wisht we had us a big looking glass. You're downright civilized again."

Lyman also studied the young man. Purified by his sweat and frigid dip, his clean blond hair shining with its fresh cut, and in good clothing, Daniel indeed had begun to look positively handsome. He was the spitting image of Rachel. Lyman figured if he could only get him to act and talk human, Daniel might be presentable enough to his mother.

"Daniel," he said, and the boy responded by looking into Lyman's eyes. "Could I get you to promise me something?"

Daniel looked at him, understanding in his eyes.

"If you promise not to try to run away, we'll not tie you up again. Even if you try to run, you won't get very far."

Daniel nodded. "Orphan not run," he said. Lyman sensed his word was to be trusted; the young man would also come to trust them sooner.

"Good. And remember that your name isn't Orphan anymore. You're Daniel. Daniel England."

Daniel's expression showed he knew the name.

"Say it, Daniel."

The boy's lips moved, trying to form the word. "Dan . . . yell."

"Good. Nate, could you-all find something to do for a while? I'd like to sit down and have a talk with Daniel. No point in starting out on the trail this late. This is a good-enough camp for another night."

"The horses need attention," John said.

"Yah, and we'd ought to see to Penn's other hosses and workin' up the packs," Nate said. "C'mon, Possum." He paused, wanting to say more. "In the mornin', Jake, I'm for makin' far-apart tracks to your cabin."

Lyman nodded. "One more day likely won't change the outcome."

The three of them trudged off to where their horses and Penn's were tied together.

"Got to see to suthin' to eat hyar pretty soon, Jake," Nate called over his shoulder. "Damn if after my bath I ain't about to take a bite out of one of them hosses' hind ends."

"Yeah, Nate," Lyman yelled after him cheerfully. "In a while." He led Daniel to a spot by the fire. Flames from the rock-heating for the lodge had dwindled; the embers had fallen in, forming a soft, glowing bed of black and grey and here and there a comforting bead of red. The deep coals radiated a mellow heat.

"We've got some things to get settled between us, son. In a couple of days I'm going to take you to your mother. She's a fine woman and I want to be sure she'll find you respectful."

Daniel looked at him as though he only half understood.

"Aim gah mo muvver."

"Back to that, eh? Try something. Say mo-ther." Lyman accentuated the sound, sticking out his tongue.

"Muv-ther."

"Mo-ther."

"Muv . . . muh-ther."

"Good. Remember how to say that. Can you say fah-ther?"

"Fav-ther. Skull fav . . . fah-ther."

"No he's not. Your father was Lieutenant Edwin England, a respected Army officer."

"Skull fah-ther," Daniel insisted. He whipped off the fur cap Lyman had given him and mussed his freshly cut hair. "Fah-ther no hair. Skull no hair. Skull fav . . . fah-ther!"

Lyman was jolted. "Judas Priest!" he said aloud, remembering what Rachel had told him of Edwin England's death. "You do remember the Indian attack!"

Daniel ran his hands around his head. "Fah-ther no hair."

"Son, your father was killed and scalped. Just because Skull has no hair doesn't make him your father. You must have seen your father's scalped body, the last thing you remember about him. Believe me, Daniel, Skull was mean and abusive to you. You must remember something about your real father. Was he ever mean to you? Like Skull was."

"Skull say Orph . . . say Dan-yell bad boy."

"Nobody's going to say that to you again, Daniel. We all think you're a good boy. No, a good man.

A hint of a smile flitted across the young man's usually stern face.

"Daniel good man today. Sit still for Jacob." He made another pass around his head with his hand to indicate his haircut. Lyman was delighted that Daniel had referred to him by name.

"And got cleaned up and into new clothes. We like Daniel now."

"Feel good, Daniel," the boy said. "Clean good. Clothes good."

"And I want you to listen to me. And to Nathan and Possum and John when we talk. Try to talk like us." He wasn't so sure that Nate's mountain jargon was such a good idea for the boy to mimic. Still it was better than the crippled English he had been using.

"Now I want to talk to you about your mother."

Lyman watched the boy intently, and saw a distinct cloud come into his eyes and into his expression. "Aim . . ."

Lyman stopped him abruptly. "Don't say that!"

"Muh-ther gone. Not come back."

"Do you remember your mother?"

"Not come back. Ain' gah no muh-ther."

"She didn't go away, Daniel. She couldn't be with you. The Indians wouldn't let her. You were taken from her. She couldn't help it."

"Muh-ther not love Daniel." He set his jaw in a childish pout.

Lyman's spirits drooped with the realization that Daniel hadn't had much chance to grow in his mind past the age of twelve or thirteen. Now, opportunities would have to be managed so he could mature in proportion to his years.

"Son, she loves you more than you'll ever know."

When they rode out next morning, Daniel went willingly, his hands free to guide his horse. Aside from Skull possibly recognizing the clothing, Lyman doubted that even Daniel's evil mentor would know his young protege.

It was the next mid-day when they rode into the clearing by the river where Lyman had killed the grizzly and saved Rachel. Strange, Lyman thought. As they neared the place, Rachel's presence grew stronger. She was everywhere around him. Indeed, he thought, she was almost close enough to hear his call.

Something inside him said she was even closer than that. She had been, ever since the night in the cabin when she had come to him and shared his bedding. Love, he thought, didn't measure distance, didn't comprehend time. It went on and there was concern, whether two people in love were apart or together. Being together made it good. Being apart could be bad, very bad.

But now she was physically close, close enough almost, to hear his shout. He looked across at the foothills, like jagged steps to the mountains beyond. Somewhere up there, on that tree-whiskered slope, was his cabin. And Rachel. His eyes hunted the hillside until he was secure that he saw and knew the area where his cabin lay hidden.

Chapter Twenty

"Jake!" Nate's tone held ominous weight, jolting Lyman out of a soft reverie. "Penn's here!" he hissed. That fast the chill air around them turned tight as cured rawhide. Lyman went stiff, his senses keen with alarm. Now he felt it too. Penn was here.

"Damn!" Lyman thought, disappointed in himself. "Once again I've underestimated our Mr. Thomas Penn. How do you suppose he got here so fast?"

"Evil men got peculiar ways, Jake," Nate said in a sort of sympathy. Nate looked at Possum. "How say, Indian? Smell. Penn here?"

Possum's mahogany features were set, wrinkled. "Smell Penn him. Not face nose smell. Other nose here smell." He pointed at his head; the sixth sense. Everyone had it, Lyman thought, amid a racing jumble of strange emotions; Indians used it best.

"I'm thinkin' he's got your woman, hoss," Chapman said.

"Then let's go get him."

"Whoa! Hold up here, Jake. We got to have a plan."

As always it was John who had the wisdom. "Nathan's right. Penn ain't going to hurt Rachel. Scare the bejeebers out of her, maybe. I know him. How he thinks. He knows if he or Skull lays a hand on her that Griz Killer Lyman won't rest until he has their heads. She's all right. Penn's fixing up a trade."

"That's right and true," Lyman said. "He's good as dead meat if he touches a hair of her head. That's the trade. What do we do?"

"I don't know that country over across there," Nate said. "We'd best get there and see what Penn's scheme is."

"You don't really know he's here."

"He's here, Jake."

"They'll both be in the cabin holding Rachel," John said. "Skull won't be out fixing a bushwhack. That'd be suicide against the four of us. Five, maybe." John glanced at Daniel.

"What about the boy?" Lyman said.

"Don't depend on him taking a hand in this," Nate said. "He don't remember his mother. Still thinks Skull's his father."

"Tie him?" John asked.

"Naw," Lyman said. "For now we've got to trust him." He paused. "All right. If they're up there. . ."

"They're up there, hoss," Chapman's voice carried an ominous tone.

"If they're up there, they're expecting us. The element of surprise is still in our favor. Won't take a few more minutes to figure all this out. Plan of attack. If they haven't hurt her, they won't before we get there."

"Any way to flank 'em, Jake?"

Lyman reflected. "I built it too good. Backs up against the mountain. Hard to approach from the sides."

"Got to go straight in," John said.

"Some of us could flank a bit on the sides. Not much." Lyman's eyes were on the forested hillside that cloaked his cabin.

"Hey, John," Nate said. "You know that slime Penn. Any chance to bargain?"

John's dark face was spread with concern. "I know the place too. Possum and me got a cabin downslope toward the river a quarter mile. You don't bargain with Penn. Got to go straight in like Jake says. Find out what Penn's game is. Right, Possum?"

The Indian was listening, taking it all in. Young Daniel England also just sat his horse and watched, his face impassive.

"No talk with Penn him," Possum said. "Penn now want to kill. All. Use woman like medicine bait. Get all to come in close. Then kill."

"Everybody's holdin' an ace," Nate said. "They got the woman. We got the boy."

"Not much to bargain with," Lyman said. "Skull's the only one who wants Daniel back. Penn hates him. We've got Penn's papers. That's what'll get him strung up. Prison, anyway. That's our ace in the hole with Thomas Penn."

"All right," Nate said. "Let's ride up there and call Penn out. Fan out and cover all his escape routes."

Jacob Lyman led out, quickly sloshing into the river and wondering at the silent, ominous calm that lay on the land; the lull before the storm. It could all erupt in a few minutes with someone's blood being spilled. Across the water, its current straining against the horse's legs, an early afternoon breeze stirred the few remaining leaves in the upstart aspens like so many wafers of pure gold.

The five riders maintained silence as the horses moved across the short span of river flats approaching the gentle rise of slopes that concealed Lyman's cabin. Lyman's eyes were busy, watching for anything unusual, any activity, any sign that would help him chart a course over the next few minutes.

At the base of the slopes, with a barely discernable path leading up into the thick trees, Nate's hand came up in a signal to halt. When his spoke, his usual loud and boastful-sounding trapper's voice turned calm, businesslike.

"Tie the pack hosses here," he said softly; they each got down and secured the animals that would only be in the way up there.

186

"John," Lyman said, "you take charge of Daniel's horse. Don't let him bolt." Old Chapman's eyes indicated agreement. They remounted and started up; Lyman felt the old apprehension building in his skin.

While they were still bunched up covering the last bit of ground to the cabin site, Nate hissed. "Dismount and tie up and spread out up there. Jake and me'll stick together at the main approach and do the talkin'."

"Maybe let them think it's just the two of us," Lyman said softly.

"Good doin's, hoss," Nate said. "Possum, you and John fan out to the sides. Keep hid unless the shootin' starts. If they come out shootin', let's hope they don't expect fire from the blind side."

When they were at last on foot, stalking the cabin, John took Daniel and disappeared to the south, while Possum scouted the north rim of the cabin bench for a likely spot to hide but still be ready for action.

Nate and Lyman separated but a few yards, near enough to see each other and give hand and facial signals. "You lead off with the talkin'," Nate whispered. "Best if they don't even know that I'm here."

They sidled easily toward the clearing that was the cabin's front yard.

At last, by poking out only part of his face around a shielding, leggy pine that had no branches below head height, Lyman could survey his home territory. Rachel's horse and two strange animals were hobbled in the broad fan of open area, nibbling at leaves and what other vegetation they could find. There was no sound. If there was any talking inside the cabin, it was muffled by the thick logs. Though he could not see smoke, Lyman could smell it as it filtered out of his natural chimney and dissipated among the uphill trees and rocks.

Possum and John, along with Daniel, were moving into position quiet as mice.

Lyman's eyes roved the scene before him once more before glancing over at Chapman, also shielded by a tree, a few feet away. Lyman darted a question with his eyes at Nate, who hunched his pegleg and stiffened his body in readiness for action and nodded. "Let's start the goddam cotillion," he whispered.

"Hello, the cabin!" Lyman bellowed. He heard alerted movement inside, maybe his bench scraping on the floor. He could see in his mind's eye Penn and Skull hustling about in sudden alarm, grabbing their rifles and crouching close to the door. A long silence, a tightness in the air, filled the time for several minutes. Penn and Skull would be quietly confirming their plan of action.

The door opened a mere crack; only enough so that words could pass clearly. "Jacob!" It was Penn's voice.

"It's me."

"Are you alone?"

"Oh, no. Not alone. Abbott and Broadus' complete brigade is with me. What there is left of them, and that's a lot. You've got no gang of bushwhackers and porkeaters and renegades to back you up this time, Penn. We fared better than you in that fight back north."

Nate winked and grinned at Lyman, acknowledging a good try at deceit.

"You lie, Jacob Lyman," Penn yelled.

"Come on out and see."

There was more silence inside the cabin as Penn chewed on that one. "I don't believe you for a minute, Jacob Lyman. Even if they are there, I can still pull your claws. We have your woman."

"That goes without saying. Send her out to me. When she's with me, you and Skull can come out. Without rifles and surely without pistols this time."

"No, we talk from here."

"Is Rachel all right?"

"The woman? It's your turn to come in and find that out for yourself."

"If you've harmed her I'll skin you alive. And there are some Indians out here who'd like to smoke Skull's hide and use it for lodge skins. No need to scrape hair."

"Big talk, Jacob. She's all right. I don't make war on women."

"When did you ever change your spots, Penn?"

Penn ignored Lyman's insinuation.

"Here's our demand. I'll have my papers and my belongings and horses you stole from me, Jacob Lyman, in your dastardly ambush of my camp the other night. Skull wants Orphan returned to him, though for the life of me I don't know why. But I go along with it. That and guaranteed safe passage out of here and no pursuit. Now isn't that a workable gentlemen's agreement? We'll take the woman with us and release her at a predetermined place."

"Faith isn't something I'm long on where you're concerned, Penn. Now here's my demands. Send Rachel out to me. Then we'll talk about letting you go."

"I have an answer for that." A rifle muzzle poked through the door's tiny opening. A cloud of smoke and belch of muzzleblast announced the bullet that spat against the tree covering Lyman. He ducked back too late, but was uninjured.

"Hunt your hole, Jake!" Nate grunted close to him. "The fight's started. Con-demned idjits!"

Lyman brushed a shard of pine bark from his cheek.

"Hold your fire, men!," Lyman commanded loudly. Nate made an acknowledging circle with a thumb and forefinger and displayed it for Lyman, grinning. Wisely Lyman saved the round in his rifle; no one else fired either.

The cabin door closed completely. Lyman's ears were pricked for any sounds that way. He felt he could hear movement in the cabin.

After what seemed an agonizingly long time, the door

again opened slightly. "You don't want my deal, Lyman, and I don't want yours. While you're thinking things over, chew on this a while."

The door opened wider and a blindfolded Rachel England was thrust out; the door partially closed again. Lyman's heart raced with emotion. Rachel's hands were tied behind her and a rope fixed around her neck. One of those inside, probably Skull, held the other end.

"Con-demned heathen Penn does make war on women and chirren," Nate said loud enough for Lyman to hear.

"Jacob," she called, her head swiveling helplessly to determine Lyman's location in her blindness. "Don't give in to him. He'll see you dead if you do!"

Lyman heard a muffled outcry inside the cabin. "Why you lowlife slut!" The rope dangling from Rachel's neck suddenly went taut and she was jerked off her feet to fall choking and gasping in the dirt at the door.

"Jake!" Nate hissed. "Don't . . ."

Lyman, ready to race to her aid in spite of Penn and Skull, checked himself with Nate's call. "Damn him," he said under his breath.

To his right, on the south slope from the cabin, Lyman heard a thrashing in the trees and brush. Young Daniel England broke out of the fringe of protective trees and began a race toward the woman slumped on the ground, trying now to bring herself to her feet.

"Mother!" Daniel screamed as he ran.

The door swung open full width and Skull stepped out beside the sprawling Rachel, bringing up his rifle. As the butt hit his shoulder, he thumbed the hammer and fired. Daniel dove in under the bullet, rolled once in his headlong race and came up again at a dead run, in a protective crouch. Skull grasped the rifle's forestock to use it as a club on the boy sprinting straight toward him.

Lyman whipped up his Hawken, taking swift aim at Skull,

and fired. In the same instant, Skull swung his rifle at the approaching Daniel. The rifle stock deflected Lyman's bullet, but the force of it destroyed Skull's aim; the arcing rifle butt whistled harmlessly over Daniel's head.

The stunning impact of Lyman's bullet on the rifle in Skull's hands spun him off-balance; he was fair game when the sledgehammer force of the speeding Daniel hit him. Daniel had tucked his head under his shoulder, and hammered Skull to the ground. They landed in a thrashing heap of struggling arms and legs.

Nate couldn't stop Lyman now. He jumped out, forgetting to reload, racing toward the cabin and the befuddled, blindfolded Rachel and the grappling Skull and Daniel.

The huge, hulking frame of Thomas Penn filled the cabin door. He brought up a loaded rifle, taking careful aim on Lyman's sprinting figure. He stepped out, shrieking, forming each word with loud and cruel emphasis. "God damn you, Jacob Lyman!"

Penn nestled his cheek against the butt and fired, and another bullet twanged in the air over Lyman's head. In reflex, as Daniel had done, Lyman dropped, lost his balance and fell roughly, but came right back up.

Apparently others thought he was hit. A giant smoke-ring of muzzle blast burst out of the trees that shielded John.

Thomas Penn took a direct hit and spun around. His momentum was stopped abruptly as he was hit again and the racing Lyman saw smoke plume up from the opposite direction where Possum had taken cover.

Penn was slammed back against the cabin, rebounded and staggered away from the walls, slumping. His toes stubbed against the now-prostrate Rachel. He fell past her, landing heavily in a dead, jumbled heap.

Daniel was having a tough time keeping the wiry, frenzied Skull from slipping out of his angry hug on the ground. Lyman dropped his empty rifle and leaped, throwing himself on the two of them. He felt another body slam into the heap and saw black arms helping to pin the furiously heaving and struggling body of the hairless man. Skull's body squirmed with mindless, frantic energy in his struggle to escape the heap of bodies suffocating him.

Another body piled on and a black braid of Possum's hair dangled past Lyman's face; underneath all of them, Skull at last lost his will to resist and lay quietly, gasping.

Amid the grunts and gasps and yells, Lyman clearly heard old Chapman's commanding voice, and all struggling stopped.

"A'right! Git off 'im. He's dead meat if he as much as tries to git off the ground until he's told. You got that, Skull?"

From his lowly position, Lyman's eyes saw a pegleg and a good leg spread in readiness, close to him, and the willing muzzle of a determined Hawken rifle. Nate Chapman stood over them, his rifle directed at the man at the bottom of the struggling mass.

The bodies lifted off Lyman and he pulled himself up stiffly. He stepped swiftly to Rachel, yanked off the blindfold and noose around her neck and unwound the thongs that bound her wrists.

He grabbed her in a frenzied embrace of relief and a great host of nameless emotions and gratitude. He felt her melting against his chest. Behind him, he heard a timid question.

"Mother? Are you my mother?"

Rachel broke from Lyman's embrace and threw herself at Daniel.

"Oh, my boy!" she sobbed. "My boy. My son. My dear, sweet son!"

For just a moment, Rachel's head swiveled toward Lyman. Standing next to the dead Thomas Penn, Jake's face shone with pride — at last he was seeing them united.

Rachel's cheeks were awash with tears. Her lips formed words that weren't uttered, but Lyman read them clearly. "Thank you, Jacob Lyman." It was all that needed to be said.

Again, the gruff mountain-man voice of Nate Chapman knifed into Lyman's racing thoughts. It occured to him that Nate was the only one left with a loaded rifle. "Well, hoss," Nate growled, but there was sarcastic triumph in the growl, "what the hell do we to with this one?"

Lyman cranked his head to see Nate holding the rifle a few inches from Skull's hairless dome. The sneak killer was whipped; his eyes were on the ground, his head hung in total defeat. Possum and John stood behind them, ready for anything if Nate lost control.

Lyman's spirits soared; he hadn't known such emotion since the grizzly was bowled over by one round from his Hawken. He had the goods on Penn, and Skull and Labelle had suffered the supreme humiliation of defeat. The crowning emotion was watching Rachel and Daniel hugging and sobbing in reunion as if tears would wash away five years of suffering and torment.

"The company's last steamboat probably hasn't gone down-river to St. Louis yet. Penn's dead so Skull will have to be made to tell what happened. With Penn's papers, Mac-Laren'll have all he needs. Get Skull manacled and sent downriver under guard. I'd be obliged if you fellas would take him out to the fort and get him on the boat. I believe just now that my place is here."

"Right on my way home to my lodge and Dawn Calf, by God!" Nate roared.

Lyman looked at Possum and John. "You two'll be heroes to the company. They may even want to send you downriver so Alexander MacLaren can personally commend you. He might even pin medals on you!"

John's teeth flashed strong, self-assured grin out of his dark face. He turned to Possum. "If we're not back before snow flies, Jacob," John said, "we'll see you in the coming-grass time. Right, Possum?"

Possum drew himself up proudly, clutching his Hawken, his smile as wide as John's.

"Skookum!" Possum said, grinning.